Sacrifice

A Story of Ancient Israel

by

J. A. Steele

For Marie-Louise

© J. A. Steele 2011

ISBN: 978-1-4467-4844-2

All Bible quotations are taken from the New International Version - Anglicised, (London: Hodder & Stoughton Ltd.) 1984, unless otherwise stated.

פ

PE

The seventeenth letter of the Hebrew alphabet

I open my mouth and pant, longing for your commands.

The sun was directly overhead. The three men had no protection from the searing heat as they carefully and quietly stacked their weapons ready for immediate use in the bottom of the ditch. They disturbed a dozing scorpion that scuttled out from under a rock and quickly found a hole in the walls of the ditch. The big man carefully eased his body up the side of the ditch and peered through the scrubby bush on its lip. He saw a gently rising slope leading to the open gate in the city walls. There were few people moving around in the heat of the midday sun, just as they had expected. He slid noiselessly back down into the ditch and whispered to his companions.

"Just a few women about. We can go straight in and out."

They nodded in agreement, and all three crept up to the lip, and over the top. Instead of running, they walked toward the gate, so that the women would not cry out until the last possible moment. They were just inside the gate when two soldiers leaped to their feet from sitting against the gatehouse: one raised a spear, but the big man parried the thrust and beheaded the soldier with a backhand stroke. He quickly turned and saw that the other was choking out his last breaths against the gate, transfixed to it by a spear. A young woman had dropped her pot and was shrieking. The wet mud showed dark against the pale red earth, as they rushed to the well and forced a goatskin flask into the bucket. There were more and more shouts now, and the flask was nearly full. The big man stopped it, and all three took to their heels, as a troop of soldiers came round the corner into the market square. They ran fast and silently through the gate and for the ditch, as arrows fell around them. The big man winced with pain as an arrow hit his back, and he nearly dropped the flask. The three slid into the ditch, snatched their own bows and felled two of the pursuers. The rest stopped and took cover. By the time their officer got them moving again, the three were well on their way.

After a few minutes they stopped to examine the big man's wound. He was suddenly conscious of the pain as his companions removed his harness. One muttered in sympathy.

"The shaft broke off in the chase, but there's a barb in there. Not deep - the leather stopped most of the way on it. Just let me cut the barb out – there you go, a good clean wound. Just think what the king will say about this - let the wounded in my service receive honour, and all that."

The big man grunted at the field surgery with a knife, but he was well accustomed to giving and receiving steel. The other's hand worked quickly and efficiently as he bound up the wound and finally gave his patient a slap on the shoulder.

"Two hours to Adullam at the most. Let's get going."

They had been walking for less than an hour when the sentry by the rock of Adullam challenged them. He was the first to hear what would soon become a much-repeated story. Word spread fast and the camp turned out in force, cheering and shouting in jubilation. The three were almost carried to the centre of the camp, where a soldier stood outside the largest of the tents.

A wiry man with a lined, weatherbeaten face emerged on a word from the soldier. He looked around with intense eyes and held up a hand for silence.

"What is that you are holding, soldier?"

The three came forward and bowed: the big man replied.

"It is a flask of water, my lord king, fresh from the well of Bethlehem by the gate."

He looked into the narrowed eyes of the king.

"So you did this because of my words this morning? When I said how I would love some of that water. Was it so?"

"It is so, lord king. Your lightest word is a command to us. And we would do more than this if you only say the word."

Eleazar shone with delight and handed over the flask to the shouts of the whole camp. He saw the king's eyes rest on the bandage round his middle, and drew himself up even taller.

David unstopped the goatskin flask. Instead of putting it to his lips, he held it out at arm's length. His wrist turned over, and the water poured out.

"God forbid that I should drink this!" he exclaimed.

"This water is as precious as the blood of these men who risked their lives to bring it to me."

Eleazar and Shammah and Josheb, the men whose blood was so precious, made no attempt to hide their astonishment. After a few moments of shocked silence, mutterings spread from man to man in the crowd, as if they could not believe what they had seen until they had described it for themselves.

The king re-entered his tent. Eleazar stood rooted to the spot while a pack donkey lapped up the water.

ג

GIMEL

The third letter of the Hebrew alphabet

Your statutes are my delight; they are my counsellors.

When the king had summoned a council of his senior soldiers and officials, there were no latecomers. Serious faces were turning this way and that in the throne room, but always with one eye on the door where the king would enter.

As it was a formal council, the throne room was lined with a double row of cedarwood chairs facing inwards. Opposite the king's throne sat the High Priest. Joab, as army commander, had a position of honour at the king's right-hand side, with Nathan the prophet about half-way down the right-hand line. Jehoshaphat took the place opposite Nathan, so as to hear everything clearly.

The king was last to enter, and opened the council without delay.

"The purpose of this council is to determine what should be done with the Ark of the Covenant. Most of you know what has happened while the Ark was being brought on its way to Jerusalem. Nonetheless, I want Joab to set out the facts of the death of Uzzah."

The general's manner was businesslike and objective.

"The Ark was in transit to Jerusalem from Baalah: it was being carried on a cart drawn by oxen. The oxen stumbled at a place called the threshing-floor of Nacon: Uzzah died on touching it."

Joab bowed his head to the king to indicate that he had finished his account: the king inclined his head in reply, and Joab sat down.

"Those are the facts. I want your advice before proceeding further about what has happened and why, and how the Ark should be treated in future."

The high priest was clearly the person addressed. He rose to address the council.

"King David, one man has died. It is certain that Uzzah committed a fault in presumptuously putting out his hand to touch the Ark. However, I do not believe that only this man was at fault."

Here he paused: a wave of the king's hand signalled that he should proceed. Nathan the prophet was silently nodding in agreement with the priest.

"The entire procedure for transporting the Ark was at fault. It was commanded to Moses that the Ark should be carried on poles of wood inserted through the carrying rings and that Levites should bear the carrying poles. Instead of the children of Levi, the tribe of priests set aside to the service of the Almighty, we have caused the Ark to be drawn on a cart by beasts of burden."

"By your permission, lord king."

Heads turned to the speaker, Seraiah, the king's secretary. Jeho noticed that Ahithopel, counsellor of the king, had tapped on the floor with a heavy wooden staff just before Seraiah had spoken. Seraiah continued.

"The high priest may we be right - indeed, I am sure he is right - in telling us that the procedure for transporting the Ark was not followed, and should have been followed. But is it necessarily the case that Uzzah was in fact struck dead by the Almighty? He was, I believe, not a strong man, and not a very healthy one either. Many men, particularly men with some weakness of body, have died from sudden shocks. Might not seeing the Ark itself slide - seeing it in danger of falling to the ground - might not that itself be a sufficient shock to kill a weak man?"

Seraiah slapped his chest to emphasise his words. David seemed unimpressed, Jeho noted, but Ahithopel inclined his head in Seraiah's direction. David continued:

"High priest, do you believe that the incident could not have happened if the correct procedure had been followed?"

"Indeed, king. The anger of the Almighty was not against one person only, but he bore the price."

"Nathan, what are we to do now? Should the Ark be left where it is?"

"No, king. All that the High Priest has said is true, and for that reason I believe that if the Ark is treated with proper reverence and dignity, it is right for it to be borne to Jerusalem, by the hands of the Levites. Know, lord king, that the Ark has been at the house of Obed-Edom for more than two months since the incident, and that his works and business have prospered as never before."

As usual, the king reached his decision without hesitation.

"Let the Ark be carried to Jerusalem as the law provides. Let the populace be gathered, and the city prepared for rejoicing and celebration."

As the priests and soldiers left the room, each with a bow to the king, Jehoshaphat automatically began his mental list of what needed to be done to implement the king's commands. It would be necessary to send messages to the Ark's resting place, to have a herald announce the entry on the eve of the event and to ensure free passage through the gates and streets of the city on the day itself, which would require instructions to close the markets.

Jehoshaphat, son of Ahilud, recorder at the court of king David, stood, moved around his stool, and bowed with respect. His bows were never perfunctory or such as to say "this is a matter of form, in fact the king needs me". The recorder had to have respect for tradition and a sense of history in order to carry out his job. Perhaps most of all, he needed a sense of duty to the generations that would come after, when David and Saul would be figures confused by inattentive children, when the cloth of the tabernacle itself would have been eaten by moths and when the words on his scrolls would have survived the dust of his bones.

In any case, the king was a man who inspired respect. Even someone who did not know about his boyhood spent in hard lying out on the hills in all weathers, about the slingshot that slew the giant of Gath, about the man who spared the life of his bitterest enemy and cut a tassel from his robe when it would have been as easy to cut his throat, who did not know about the spilled water from the well of Bethlehem, even one who had not heard the poems – even someone who knew nothing of David would have been able to see that he was someone used to being obeyed, and someone men would follow anywhere.

"What did you think of that meeting, Jeho?"

Jeho wondered how candid the king expected him to be.

"I think, lord king, that the words of the holy men cannot have come as a surprise to you."

"Of course not. I know where we went wrong. If a man scalds himself he doesn't need to be told it's because the water was hot. So why did I summon them all, then, if I already knew?"

"So that everyone else knows that you know. So that Joab and the other commanders understand."

"And so that they know that I consult the holy men when it matters. Correct. This is why I need you, Jeho. And now you will make a note of that meeting and add it to the records."

Jeho bowed to make his departure.

"One more thing. I want you to be present and record some discussions with the ambassadors from Lebanon: since you were at the talks in Tyre, they'll have confidence in you. They are staying at the house of Ahithopel. Go and pay your respects to them tomorrow."

In his work-room Jeho cut himself a new stylus while a servant mixed the ink to the right consistency. He recorded the meeting on a sheet of parchment, and left it to one side to dry. That task completed, he went down to the courtyard to see the guard squad at their exercise.

The captain of the king's bodyguard, Benaiah, was a man of many excellent qualities. He was of course a great warrior. His kills included a lion and an Egyptian giant whom he had killed with his own spear after taking it from his hand. Even more important, perhaps, the King trusted him implicitly. More so, even, than Joab, the commander of the army.

Benaiah enjoyed his drills (he could routinely place three spears within a hand's breadth of each other at seventy paces) and especially sword practice, although there were few sparring partners to match him. The elite warriors of David's army – the Thirty – contained almost the only ones who could test him. However, in addition to the Thirty there was the even more select group – the Three. This afternoon's practice was against Eleazar, his favourite opponent.

They each selected one of the wooden practice swords, and took position in the ring. They circled warily for a few seconds before Eleazar launched the first attack with a lunge to Benaiah's throat. He arrested the movement before it was complete – a feint designed to make Benaiah commit himself and draw his sword upwards. As the real stroke came in for his midriff, Benaiah was slightly too late to block the move completely and Eleazar's wooden sword scraped the skin off his right knee. He nodded in acknowledgement of the hit.

The next opponent was a lean, intense-looking man with long black wavy hair. He charged into Benaiah with a whirlwind of blows on each side of the helmet and shoulders, driving him back with the reckless velocity of the assault. Parrying and retreating at once, Benaiah lost his footing and stumbled onto one knee. That changed the course of the bout, as Benaiah's opponent lost his momentum, and stood still for a breath to draw back his sword for a decisive thrust. In that moment Benaiah grabbed his wrist with his own left hand and pulled him forwards off balance and down onto the packed earth. Then Benaiah's sword was at his opponent's neck and the bout was over.

The defeated warrior refused to stay for a cup of wine with the rest of the captains, and came in for some chaffing about his devotion to his wife.

"Don't be late, Uriah!"

"Bathsheba will attack you with her skillet – and she'll be tougher than Benaiah!"

The soldiers invited Jeho to join them for their wine, and in the heat of the afternoon they settled under an awning in a corner of the courtyard. Jeho was not quite one of them, but like all Hebrew men he bore arms when required: there was a mutual respect among them.

Eleazar pulled up a stool for the recorder, and poured him a cup of a sweet red wine, which Jeho watered generously.

"Tell me, then, Eleazar," asked Jeho, "what did I miss at the valley of Rephaim?"

"You missed a good fight there, Jeho. Why were you not there; the king led us in person?"

"I was with King Hiram that day, not King David. I had a mission to Tyre."

Eleazar knew better than to ask for more details of a diplomatic mission.

"The Philistines had just taken one beating at Baal Perazim, and then they came back to Rephaim. I think that was their mistake."

Eleazar leaned back and took a gulp of wine.

"Not so, Eleazar."

Benaiah was frowning thoughtfully.

"A defeat can be the best time to strike back, especially if the other side is over-confident, thinking they won't see you again for a long time. Coming straight back after a defeat can be a real surprise. I have known a campaign turn on that sort of initiative."

There were one or two murmurs of agreement round the table, but Eleazar was unimpressed.

"Perhaps, on some occasions, but it didn't do the Philistines any good that day. They were in position by the wood in the Valley of Rephaim. Do you know the place?"

"Yes, I think so. Isn't it a wood of mulberry trees?"

"Yes, mulberry trees. Anyway, the king led us around the edge of the forest instead of coming straight on towards them." His satisfaction was evident. "Then there was a long wait for the word to attack. But David timed it just right in the end - I would have gone sooner - and we wiped out the Philistines; all the way down to Gezer we chased them."

"The King gets most things right," said Benaiah.

"He usually manages to be in the right place at the right time and to pick the right moment."

Most of the men around the table nodded.

"He is anointed," said one of the men - a heavily-built man Jeho had seldom set eyes on before.

"That means that he is chosen to lead us to victory."

"Not necessarily," Eleazar said. "Saul was anointed too, and look how he finished up."

There was a grim laugh from most of those present, in which Benaiah did not join.

Another man - Zelek - seemed not to notice that Benaiah's temper was rising, and carried on, "Some people say that what Samuel does with his oil flask is one thing and what the Everlasting wills is another. Not everyone accepts that David is truly fit to be king over Israel. He has fought in the service of the Philistines, it is rumoured."

Jeho had to put the record straight on this point.

"In fact it is not a rumour. He fought in the service of Achish, the king of Gath. But he did not fight against Israelites. Those he fought were the enemies of the people of Judah."

Benaiah burst out, "That's right, Jehoshaphat! I won't hear a word against the King. I am the King's man. What the King wants, the King gets. God is with him. I am with the King."

Jehoshophat frowned in the shade.

"The King has the duty to go with God, not the contrary. It is written of Joshua, that before the battle of Jericho he went to see the lie of the land. There he met a mighty man, and asked him whether he was for Joshua and the Israelites, or for the Canaanites. But the man was the angel who commands the armies of the Lord. The question was whether Joshua was on his side, not the other way round."

Benaiah looked as if he was suddenly tired of the conversation. He said something about inspecting the guard, and stood up to go. The party began to break up.

Jeho watched Benaiah's purposeful stride as he went away: it reminded him of his brother. His death in battle was a wound that still hurt Jeho. He wondered if he would survive the wars that seemed such an inescapable part of life.

Jehoshaphat returned to his work-room to retrieve the parchment he had written earlier, and take it to the archives. The archives were stored in a long, narrow, low-ceilinged room on the ground floor of the palace. It was lit by a series of narrow windows or rather slits opening onto an inner courtyard. It would have been impossible to keep rats from the sheepskin without storing the scrolls in wooden trunks supported on stone blocks. Jehoshaphat went along the room to the trunk containing his current texts, and placed the scroll inside it.

Jehoshaphat started to close the lid of the cedarwood trunk. His eye rested lovingly for a second on the collection of scrolls it contained. There's one thing we do well, he thought, and that is to remember. Stories, cairns, genealogies, tombs – so much that is a part of our lives to keep us from forgetting. We have to know who we are, where we come from. Unlike the Egyptians who are so concerned with where they are bound to, so fixed on their journey to the Far Horizon that they spend half their lives planning to die. We want to remember where we came from, what covenant we have with the Everlasting.

Jehoshaphat's ambition was to complete and maintain a chronicle commencing with the birth of Samuel and continuing throughout the reigns of Saul and David. He had many more urgent tasks as court recorder, but none more important than transmitting to the later generations the story of how the kingdom came into being. It was a story of a stubborn people, of an inspired prophet, of a tortured king, reluctant at first, then arrogant and finally despairing, of a shepherd boy anointed by a prophet and of a friendship unbroken by war and death. It was not yet written, and perhaps Jehoshaphat would not complete it, but he could certainly write enough to point the way.

He closed the lid, and his fingers brushed the cedarwood.

ד

DALETH

The fourth letter of the Hebrew alphabet

*I have chosen the way of truth; I have set my heart on
your laws.*

Jeho was stopped on the way out of the palace: Caleb blocked the
petitioner but Jeho waved her through. She was about twenty-
five, with impassioned flashing eyes and a deep voice. She
clearly had no time to waste.

"My lord Jehoshaphat, a great injustice is about to be
committed. I plead with you to speak words of justice and mercy
in the ear of the King so that I and my family will not be
destroyed by the plots of evil men!"

Jehoshaphat was immediately interested, not only by the content
of the message but by the manner of the messenger. She
reminded him of someone, although he had a vague sense that
the physical appearance was not a close match.

"Please, lady, tell me the facts of the matter, starting from the
beginning."

She collected herself and concentrated. "My name is Marion,
daughter of Helek. My sister Zilpah is betrothed to Shimron, son
of Jehu. Shimron owns some plots of land, not of very great use
or value for the most part. But he also owns a vineyard which
borders on the vineyards of that great man Ahithopel."

Jeho groaned silently. Any case involving the interests of
Ahithopel would be vigorously contested on one side at least, and
by the sounds of it, his suppliant was on the other side.

"Ahithopel has coveted Shimron's vineyard for many years. He has offered twice the worth of it but Shimron refuses to sell. So now Ahithopel has decided to remove him by using the law as his weapon. He has laid a trap to compass my family's shame and ruin, in order to gain his vineyard!"

"How exactly is this trap to work, lady?"

"He plans to have us killed for breaking the law. The law condemns to death those found to have committed adultery. Ahithopel seeks my death and Shimron's too. I am certain that Ahithopel has bribed my household servants to testify against us."

She was, Jeho realised, completely unafraid. She was bold and looked him fearlessly in the eye, but without even being aware of her boldness. Her attention was fixed on him and how he reacted rather than on herself: that was why he found her a little disconcerting.

"This is a serious charge to make against Ahithopel. You must know that he is one of the King's most trusted counsellors."

"It is the truth."

Jeho challenged her.

"Tell me the truth: have you lain with Shimron?"

Marion looked away from his face for the first time in the conversation: "I have not lain with Shimron. It is the truth."

"Go now. I shall consider this matter."

As she turned to go Jeho realised why her eyes were so striking: she had made them up with a little downward flick in the corner by her nose and an upward one in the other corner. But there was more to it than make-up: it was her whole attitude that gave her such a presence.

Her lack of modesty should not be held against her in the circumstances: it could be attributed to her passion and fear, thought Jeho. Marion's story might well be true. All cases are straightforward, he knew, if one has heard only one side of the story. He had said he would consider the matter and had sent her on her way: now he had to decide whether to cross swords with one of the most prominent men in Jerusalem.

If this case was as she had stated it and if it came before the king it would mean two deaths. There was only one verdict the king could reach on those facts; quite apart from the fact that Ahithopel was the king's most respected counsellor. There were many reasons not to cross him. He was powerful and influential. The king had ordered Jeho to cooperate with Ahithopel on the matter of the reception of the ambassadors from Lebanon. A dispute with Ahithopel would certainly make it more difficult to serve the king as he liked to be served.

However, the case might not have to come to court. There might be a way to stop the case from grinding its way to a conclusion in front of the king's throne. He needed to find out more about the matter at dispute.

Jeho and Caleb made their way slowly through the crowded streets, Caleb shouting "Make way" at regular intervals to no noticeable effect. They passed a spice seller whose goods made Jeho catch his breath with delight. The spice seller saw his reaction and held a handful of sumac under his nose, and the sweet tangy smell of the crushed berries was hard to resist. They passed by an open housefront where a weaver was making a carpet, with the shuttle flying over the loom as the pattern built up row by row. He had to stop at the perfumer's, and after sampling various products bought a delicate jar of rose-petal oil for Deborah. Most of the time involved in the process was taken up by Caleb's haggling over the price with the perfumer. Caleb had a bargaining ritual which Jeho always enjoyed, although from behind an impassive face so as not to undermine his slave's histrionic performance. The ritual involved professions of friendship, admiration of the goods which was then tempered by the sudden discovery of a flaw or recollection of a cheaper equivalent elsewhere, sarcastic laughs and usually a sudden turn to depart. Because the vendor was equally proficient in the grammar of bargaining the performance took some time.

TETH

The ninth letter of the Hebrew alphabet

Do good to your servant according to your word, O LORD.

Like most wealthy Hebrews, Jeho had a house in Jerusalem as well as his country estate. It was not very long since the city had been captured from the Jebusites. Jeho's house had belonged to a Jebusite lord with poor taste in statues and interior decoration, but Jeho and Deborah had been able to change it in accordance with their tastes. It was built around a central courtyard, where Caleb rebuked a serving girl who was chatting idly to a lounging youth.

Deborah had brought an unusually rich dowry to their marriage. She had been orphaned and was the sole inheritor of her mother's father's lands. This had given her an unusual degree of independence and she had been able to marry according to her own choice. Since the settlement of Canaan, the Hebrews had made the transition from measuring wealth in terms of cattle to measuring it by land. Jeho's lands were mostly pasture country in the Jordan valley, but he also had some orchards and vineyards bought by his father.

Jeho reflected that it was not so very difficult to get wealth, but much more difficult to hold on to it. The Hebrews were in a more or less constant state of war. That meant spoils for the conquerors but it could also lead to whole families being wiped out. In peacetime sons bury fathers and in wartime fathers bury sons. Perhaps one day there would be a time of stability, but until then it was a struggle to hold what they had.

Deborah was sitting on a couch in the reception room with a bowl of grapes on a low table, her writing equipment spread out

18

before her. She put down her pen to greet Jeho, taking care not to stain her garment. He could see that she had noticed the little jar: he was pleased to think that she was just as excited as when she received her first present from him.

The gift was a clear success: her eyes opened wide and she breathed in the perfume deeply. After a second intake of breath she closed the jar and embraced Jeho.

Dinner consisted of roasted ribs of lamb, delicately flavoured with cumin, followed by honey-cakes and small oranges.

Caleb lit a pair of lamps and left the couple in privacy. Jeho poured wine and watered it for both of them. Deborah sipped her wine reflectively.

"I went to the palace today myself."

Jeho had the impression that Deborah's casualness was assumed. "I suppose you were seeing Michal."

"Yes. Or the queen, I suppose we should say. She gets very angry and bitter these days. Sometimes she refers to herself sarcastically as the queen."

"Is that because of Abigail?"

Deborah nodded in a distant sort of way, looking into the lamplight.

"Don't you even think of getting another wife. I want you all to myself. Especially when I see how eaten up with jealousy Michal is."

"Her father really destroyed her life. And a lot of other peoples' lives as well. I think you're one of the few who continues to have time for Michal, even though she may be the king's wife. Everyone in the palace can tell she's on the way down in the king's affections since Abigail came."

"Sometimes what everyone knows is not the truth. I think that David still loves Michal, in a way."

Jeho thought that Deborah was probably right about that point. "For one thing, she is Jonathan's sister. That family touched David in very many ways."

Deborah reached for a bowl of nuts. "The man Saul gave Michal to - Palti - is he still alive?"

"As far as I know. Obviously a lot of Saul's men died at the end, but I don't remember hearing anything of him."

Deborah's mind was moving on.

"You can't really work with someone well if you don't like him, can you?"

Jeho frowned. "You're still thinking of Ahithopel - I wonder if there's some connection between Seraiah and Ahithopel, by the way. I wouldn't like to think that I can only work with people I don't dislike. It's a matter of duty. If I can best serve the king by talking to someone I disapprove of that's what I have to do."

A smile spread over Deborah's face. "You're not a hypocrite, Jeho, and that's one of the things I love about you. I wonder if others can see as clearly as I can when you don't like someone."

Jeho hoped not. An official, especially one with ambassadorial duties, should be able to conceal at least some of his reactions.

She swallowed a nut and changed the subject suddenly.

"Why are you seeing the men from Lebanon tomorrow? Is it about the temple?"

"Don't let it be widely known. If people know about it in Jerusalem, people will know about it in Tyre, and we'll find prices going up."

"I say that the tent was good enough for Moses and Aaron, for Joshua and for Gideon. When we were in the wilderness the pillar of cloud and fire moved on and the people had to move with it or die in the wilderness. Will the glory of the Lord consent to take root in a building of stone?"

Deborah rarely talked like that, but Jeho understood that there were some things she would fight a lion to defend. That was part of what he loved about her. The aristocratic lady he had married, at ease in the king's court, had a fierce combativeness in her, like Miriam or Jael.

"You know what I want. I want to serve the king: that's what I do when I get up in the morning, when I go to the palace. But I want to help him make something that counts for the service of the Everlasting. I tried to explain that to Benaiah today but I don't think he understood. He's just loyal to the king. That's the beginning and end of it."

"What does this woman - Marion - what does she want you to do?"

"She wants me to intervene with the king on her behalf."

He quickly told her Marion's story. Deborah looked thoughtful.

"Do you think she has lain with this Shimron?"

"She says not, but she had a shifty look about her while she was saying so. Having said that, I have a feeling she might have been telling the truth about that specific question, but that there is something else she wasn't prepared to reveal."

"Such as an affair with someone other than Shimron?"

"Perhaps. Just a guess."

"I wish I'd seen her. I'd have been able to tell. Will you intervene for her?"

"The problem is, it will mean placing myself in opposition to Ahithopel. Perhaps it's time to do that. If a man chooses his friends carefully, he should choose his enemies even more carefully."

Deborah smiled lightly.

"You think in those terms so habitually that I don't think you know you're doing it. Court politics, who's up, who's down, who's the next ambassador to Egypt..."

"You never object to hearing about it."

Even so, Jeho realised that she had a point: he had just been talking about Michal being on the way down.

"I suppose you're right. No sign of Ahithopel going down, though. It's a mystery to me why the king places such trust in a man who is so different from him."

"Perhaps that's why. He needs him to think the thoughts he can't think himself. Just as you need me to fill in the gaps in your thinking."

Jeho gave Deborah a severe look and cracked into a grin when he saw the expression on her face.

"I think you should show more respect to the king's recorder. David takes notice of what I say even if you don't."

Deborah nodded sagely.

"What you do is the part that lasts, isn't it?" Deborah said.

"I mean to say, what remains to us of our ancestors, more than the records, that make sense of everything else that comes down? Like the Ark - it contains Aaron's staff, but what would that matter if we didn't know who Aaron was, who Moses was, and what they did?"

"The records are very important for that reason, but they're not the only thing. After all, the main thing that remains of our ancestors is we ourselves. The other main thing is the starting position we inherit from them - like the fact that we're here in Canaan and not in Egypt."

They both fell silent and reflected on the legacy for which they had no heir.

Jeho took up the theme again.

"But I agree with you about the importance of selecting the right things to record. For instance, just paying attention to something once – that's enough to take something out of the general run of events. If you tell someone else about it, then it's well out of the commonplace. Finally, at the extreme, you can set up a stone or something like that. Before Caleb left us just now, for instance, he went over to the lamp in the window and checked how much oil was in it. He decided there was enough and went out. But he delayed at the window for a moment, looking at something in the street. He probably hardly thought at the time about what he was doing and by now he has forgotten it. I hardly noticed him, but now I've told you I shall remember that moment longer than I would otherwise have done. "

Deborah frowned slightly.

"Well of course - each of us at every moment is surrounded by any number of things we could attend to but in general we don't. We just concentrate on what's important to us."

"Exactly. You said it. What's important to us. Because it works the other way as well. What we ignore now is lost to the future."

Deborah was ready for bed: she blew out one lamp, picked up the other and made her way towards the chamber door.

"I wonder who's occupying your mind at this moment, Jeho. I hope it isn't Caleb."

ח

HETH

The eighth letter of the Hebrew alphabet

At midnight I rise to give you thanks for your righteous laws.

Michal was alone in bed, as she often was these days. She had been the first woman that David had taken to wife, but she was not the last. She knew it would be fatal to try to make him choose between her and Abigail; she had no confidence that she would win if she forced the issue. She must at least preserve a facade of cordiality with Abigail.

King Saul had promised Michal to whoever could kill Goliath and when David defeated the Philistine Michal became his, although he had had to pay an additional bride-price of a hundred Philistine foreskins. She had expected to be given to some grizzled captain, and as a young man David was more of a companion than her lord and master, at least in the early years of their marriage. During the years of Saul's enmity with David, she had been given in marriage to a man called Palti, who could not compare with David.

Abigail had had a husband before David. She had been married to a man called Nabal, who had benefited from the protection of David's warriors. David had later asked him for food and been refused, and David and his warriors were on the way to punish him when Abigail, whose servants had warned her that David was on his way, had gone out to meet him with a large store of supplies loaded on donkeys. She had bowed down to the ground before David and asked for mercy. Later, after Abigail had told her husband about her encounter with David, Nabal suffered a stroke and died. David had then asked Abigail to become his wife. The name Nabal meant fool: he might have been one, but Abigail was a shrewd woman who could act decisively.

Michal had no way of knowing if things would have turned out the same had she still been David's wife at the time he met Abigail. Since David had taken another wife before Abigail, it might well have been so. Nonetheless, Michal had never forgiven her father Saul for passing her on to another man in marriage.

When David had assumed the throne, he demanded the return of Michal. Was it only to satisfy his injured pride, or had he continued to love her, and wish for her companionship? Whatever David's feelings for Michal were, there was one inescapable fact: Abigail had given David a son and Michal had not.

"David, David," she muttered softly. "Are you with her now?" She got out of bed and draped a shawl over her shoulders, and leaned on her balcony to watch the moon rise over Jerusalem. She thought of Jonathan her brother, and of how she missed his open cheerful face, his dauntless courage and generous nature. She had not forgotten how he drove her wild with frustration as a child because he would, she believed, sooner have died than admit himself to be in the wrong. He had faced down his father in the same way, even when Saul was king. No-one ever got the better of Jonathan. Until, one day, the Philistines did so on Mount Gilboah, when father and son died in the same battle. She was used to death and loss, like everyone else, but the loss of her brother would hurt her forever. Now she was losing that brother's closest friend, her husband.

"David, how can I win you back to my side, dear David?" Her balcony overlooked the narrow Kidron valley and the road that snaked up to the gates. A three-quarters full moon washed the scene with a pale light, and she could see a fox snuffling around on the other side of the valley. In the intensity of her feelings of longing, regret and frustration, she could imagine herself leaping from the balcony, transformed into a night hunter, snuffling out small mammals and running mile after mile through trees and rocks lit by the pale moon. Even while she indulged the wild fantasy she knew that in the real world it would be hard for her even to slip on a cloak and shoes and to walk out of the palace. At this time of night the guards would not allow a wife of the king to come and go as she wished. They would send for the chamberlain and he would ask her question after question, but she would not get out of the palace.

Palti had loved her at least. He had been besotted by her. She had gone unwillingly to his house - Saul had treated her like a chattel. But Palti had thrown all dignity to the winds over her, weeping and wailing in public when David took her back. If only some of Palti's craving for her could have rubbed off onto David!

Her thoughts turned to the note she had received that evening. The note had been delivered by a slip of a serving-girl with a heavy veil, who had refused to give it into any hands except Michal's. When she saw the note she understood why. It was a request from Ahithopel for her to wait on him at his house the next day. At first she had been minded to refuse out of hand because of his presumption, but then she had reflected with chagrin that she might need powerful allies at court if she was to regain any influence with the king. At least, she had no need of more enemies.

If I gave David a son, she said to herself, her thoughts moving in to the subject that was never far from the front of her mind. If I gave him a son his love for me would burn as bright as in the beginning. There might be a way. It was utterly abhorred by the priests, but they were all men. She had heard - as everyone had - of the queen of heaven, giver of increase. It was rumoured that there were places near the city, high places where the queen of heaven received the honour she deserved, and that those who honoured her received her gift of increase. The prophets often condemned the high places and the Asherah poles, but they never had to explain what they were. They were part of the background of life in Canaan from before the time of the Hebrews, and she did not expect them to disappear for a long time yet.

Eleazar had seen the same moon rise near the end of his journey. He had assumed the task of going to the house of Obed-Edom with the news about the Ark's next journey. He had volunteered partly because he liked the idea of riding a good horse on a road he knew well, but also to take a look at the Ark itself, or at least the tent where it was kept. After greeting Obed-Edom, pausing only to give the groom orders about rubbing down the horse, he passed on the king's instructions about the Ark. It was to be carried only by Levites, however short the distance it was being moved, and only on carrying poles placed through the rings. Obed-Edom did not need to be told: Uzzah's death had made a deep impression on him.

Eleazar approached the tent with his usual brisk stride, but slowed down as he got nearer to it. He stopped just within the boundary and stood for a hundred breaths reflecting on the Ark. God had told Moses how to build the Ark, how to consecrate it and how to shield it from view. God had sent the cloud to direct the ways of the Hebrews and all had led to this place at this moment.

Like all Hebrews Eleazar knew what the Ark contained: his father had taught him about the staff, the jar and the tablets of stone. Food for the body, a law to obey and a reminder of the power of the Almighty to bring life out of death.

QOPH

The nineteenth letter of the Hebrew alphabet

I rise before dawn and cry for help; I have put my hope in your word.

Caleb brought them a plate with two loaves, made the previous evening, and a bowl of curds. Deborah waited for Jeho to speak the words of blessing over the food.

"Blessed are you, Lord our God, King of the Universe, who brings forth bread from the earth."

He was as usual formally dressed with a brightly coloured robe over his linen tunic. The robe was made of red silk with blue fringes and gold tassels.

When the meal was over, Jeho and Caleb set out for the day's business.

"What do you know about Ahithopel, Caleb?"

"I know he's rich. He has a lot of slaves, but he never sells any. If he buys you, you'll only leave the house feet first, they say."

Jeho wondered why that might be. Perhaps a man with a lot of secrets might want to keep his household under tight control. On the other hand, the fewer slaves, the easier it would be to keep them tightly enclosed.

"Another thing about him - he has a beautiful granddaughter who got married to Uriah the Hittite."

Jeho remembered the soldier who had been taunted for his devotion to his wife. It sounded as thought she might be worth his devotion.

Jeho was determined not to allow the Shimron matter to dominate his thoughts as he dealt with Ahithopel. His first duty was to the king and his business, and today that meant the ambassadors.

The door keeper had been told to expect them and let them in almost before Caleb had stated Jeho's name.

Jeho and Caleb entered the house of Ahithopel. The house had a richness and depth about it, in its cedar and acacia furnishings, patterned carpets in red and purple and turquoise, glints of silver from its hanging lanterns. There were metal grilles on the windows as well as wooden shutters, open now in the mid-morning, making hexagonal patterns of light on the walls.

There were, as Caleb had hinted, more servants than he had ever seen in a private house before: they lined the walls and made gestures of obeisance as Jehoshaphat was led through the entry hall to the reception room. Ahithopel's butler seated Jehoshaphat on a couch, clearly expecting Caleb to stand behind his master and look for gestures. The butler summoned a serving-girl who poured wine and presented it to Jeho. Both left them alone. Turning slightly, Jeho could see that his servant was looking after the departing figure of the serving-girl with admiration.

"Do you admire the woman, Caleb?"

"Well, Master Jeho, I have to say that she's the most mouth-watering sight I've seen since last night's dinner."

"That is the point, Caleb. You see her in that way because she intends you to do so, and that is how she sees herself."

"What do you mean, how she sees herself?"

"I mean that she can only understand herself in the light of her attractiveness to men. It is not her fault - that is all she has ever been shown."

Caleb seemed unconvinced but disinclined to continue the discussion. They waited in silence: Jehoshaphat suspected that the wait was intended to prove a point.

29

The butler returned, opening a double door for the master of the house. Jeho rose to his feet: Ahithopel waited to install himself on a couch before inviting Jeho to resume his seat. He leaned forward, both hands clasped around the top of his staff, the foot of which rested on the floor between his feet.

"Your visit is most welcome, Jehoshaphat. I thank you for the honour you grant to my poor dwelling."

"The honour is all mine, counsellor. I thank you for the warmth of your welcome."

Jeho studied the man opposite him. His face was pinched and long, almost cadaverous as it ran down to his pointed chin. The face was no more than a frame for the two intense, almost reptilian eyes that held his unblinkingly.

"The king has, I believe, requested that you join me in welcoming the ambassadors from Tyre?"

Jehoshaphat was slightly surprised to be getting down to business so quickly: he had expected many more courtesies to be exchanged before starting work.

"Indeed so, counsellor. You may recall that I attended the court of king Hiram recently. King David wishes me to make a record of the discussions with the ambassadors. Is there anything I should know before meeting them?"

"I should appreciate a word in your private ear, recorder."

Jeho inclined his head and Caleb slipped out silently with a bow that took in both men. He knew how to be respectful when necessary.

מ

MEM

The thirteenth letter of the Hebrew alphabet

I have more understanding than the elders, for I obey
your precepts.

Ahithopel laid his staff on the table between them, but slightly to
one side.

"Let us talk about the Ark, recorder. Why, do you think, has our
king David brought the Ark here?"

"Because the Ark is where we are – the children of Israel. It is
the sign that the Almighty has given us prophets, His law, His
sustenance. Do the Ammonites have an Ark? Do the Philistines?
They have gods of stone and wood: we have a sign of the glory of
the Lord."

Jeho was watching intently for Ahithopel's reaction, and both of
them knew it. The long impassive face gave nothing away as the
counsellor shrugged.

"It is certain that the Ark is important; but why is it here?
Jerusalem is not anywhere of any significance."

"Say rather, it has not been a place of any significance. Now it
is. And it will be more so. For one thing, Jerusalem is defensible.
It lies in the Judean mountains, and that suits our kind of
fighting. It has valleys on both sides of the ridge. It was hard for
David to capture from the Jebusites, and we'll make sure it's even
harder for anyone else to take."

"Indeed. A city whose name is peace, taken by us in war."
Ahithopel picked a grape off the silver platter between them. He

rolled it in his fingers first one way, then the other, then popped it into his mouth.

"Let us speak about the temple, recorder. Will it be built, some day soon?"

"Certainly it will be built, but not in one day, and not in one year either. But the question is, when will the work start? When people see the ground being cleared, stones being shaped, pillars fitted together - at that point it becomes more than an idea."

"Do you then believe, recorder, that the temple must be built? Can you imagine that we would not survive without it?"

"That is what all other nations around us have – and we don't. A temple."

"True enough. And what is it they can do that we can't? We can't burn our children to death for Moloch, for example, or couple with prostitutes to worship Ashera. We have rules to live by and a practice that reminds us we are bound to the Everlasting. He has a covenant with us. That is better than the biggest temple on earth. "

"Some people say that the tent was good enough for Moses and Aaron, for Joshua and for Gideon. They say that when we were in the wilderness the pillar of cloud and fire moved on and the people had to move with it or die in the wilderness. Will the glory of the Lord consent to take root in a building of stone?" He was consciously repeating his wife's words, which had impressed themselves on him.

"Indeed, some reason so. Our lord the king, recorder, is a man of noble motives. There are others, however, whose minds dwell on worldly matters, like how much work is involved in bringing the forests of Lebanon to Mount Zion."

"And on how much gold has to change hands to make that work happen. Your point is not lost on me." Jeho thought how much like talking to the king this conversation was. Ahithopel had the same acuteness and unexpectedness that David had.

"I am thinking of war, recorder, and in particular that it is a poor way to allocate wealth."

"What do you mean, a way to allocate wealth? War has to do with death and destruction."

"Let me make myself clear, recorder. Suppose you want to have ..." Ahithopel glanced about and his eyes fixed on the cup in Jeho's hand, "that cup you hold. How can you acquire it? One method would be to beat me senseless and run away."

Jeho gave a little laugh, and Ahithopel fixed him with his gleaming eyes. "You laugh at the idea, recorder, because for a man in your position that would not be a productive strategy. What would you do instead?"

"Well, I could ask you to sell it to me, of course."

"Of course. So we see that trade and violence are two alternative strategies. Why do I say that war is less effective? Because its effects are less certain."

Jeho felt that he was completely losing control of the conversation.

"Let me see if I follow you. Trade has a cost, of course, because I have to give you something in order to get the thing I want. But war has a cost as well: the king has to pay his soldiers, feed and equip them and so on."

"You understand me very well. The point about war is that the costs are certain but the benefits very uncertain. You can invest heavily and lose everything."

"True - but the same applies to trade, especially over the seas."

"To some extent, that is so. But in general the returns from trade are more certain than those from fighting."

Jeho was beginning to wonder if Ahithopel was making a covert criticism of the king. If so, why to him? Could Ahithopel be sounding him out?

"I can agree with you on that. It is better for all concerned if we can get cedar from Lebanon by trade rather than war. But not all wars are wars of choice. If your enemy comes over your borders and steals and plunders, a king has to react with his own army. The calculation of whether to fight is not his."

"Now it is my turn to agree with you, recorder. The calculation has to be made by the king who will take the initiative, as in so many other areas. The first question is whether to move at all."

As Ahithopel gazed up he had the appearance of someone who was truly noble, thought Jeho. Ahithopel continued. "The most important thing in life, recorder, is to conquer one's own lower nature. When ignorance and passion hold sway, no clear and elevated thoughts, words or actions are possible."

Jeho felt unsure about this. "When the lower nature is conquered, what does one go on to do then?"

Ahithopel smiled tightly. "It is the work of a lifetime, recorder."

Ahithopel had been moving his hands about while he spoke, but now stopped stock still, fixing Jeho in the eye.

"The king has requested us to work together, recorder. Can we do so, do you think?"

Jeho took the plunge. "Do you know of a man called Shimron?"

"Indeed I do. He is a neighbour of mine: at least, he owns some land adjoining my estate. Do you know Shimron?"

"No, I do not. But one of his kinsfolk has made some representations to me in the matter of Shimron's vineyard."

"Let me be frank with you, Jehoshaphat. I should like to own Shimron's land. I have made offers to him, and generous offers at that. I do not think that he or his kinsfolk should have cause to complain on that account."

"If he has received an open and generous offer, Ahithopel, then indeed he should have no cause to complain. I have been asked to intervene in a matter concerning adultery."

"That is none of my concern, Jehoshaphat. And, I hope, none of yours either. "

Jeho smiled faintly. "As you say."

"We both want the same thing, recorder. We both want a strong kingdom, under a strong king, with its royal city here in Jerusalem. Do I say too much?"

Jeho shook his head.

"In that case, I look forward to our cooperation in the dealings with the ambassadors from Lebanon, and in other matters."

"I am certain that we can cooperate on the king's business, Ahithopel."

Their eyes met. Neither man blinked, and neither had the least illusion but that their emnity had been declared.

The meeting with the ambassadors allowed the tension to dissipate, or, at least, to be kept under a veneer of cordiality.

The ambassadors were both tall and heavy men with long black wavy hair: they might have been easy to confuse with each other if they had been of similar ages. The senior ambassador was at least ten years older than his colleague.

Ahithopel served a deep rich red wine from some island: it must have cost more for a flask than Jehoshaphat had paid for his coat. Jeho wondered how much Ahithopel really appreciated the wine: he didn't look like a man who enjoyed any physical pleasures very much. Perhaps he bought the best wines to show how successful he was, and what good taste he had. Jeho realised at this point that his dislike of Ahithopel could easily affect his judgment.

They spoke of Tyre, and that led to forests and that led to trees, and how the finest trees were much appreciated all over the world and how much the Hebrews appreciated the cedars of Lebanon.

It was late afternoon by the time they left Ahithopel's house: the sudden shock of sunlight was refreshing after so much time indoors. Adjusting to the light in the street outside, Jeho had to admit to himself that Ahithopel had handled the meeting very diplomatically. He had let Jeho take a central position in the meeting and had acted as a gracious host.

"Caleb – where did they take you to wait for me?

"Back to the room where we waited before, master. The serving girl we saw before came back with a flask of wine."

"Very generous. Did you notice anything unusual while you were waiting?"

"Out of the way, there!" This was addressed to a man driving a donkey down the middle of the narrow street. "No. She asked about you and the mistress – what you were like to work for, what food I got, that sort of thing."

Jeho turned sideways, trying to get past the donkey without dirtying his robes against the wall.

"I see. Do you think she came to see you for the pleasure of your company, or could she have been ordered to, perhaps?"

Caleb shot him a grin.

"I'm sorry to say, Master Jeho, that the same question came to me. I think the girl doesn't have enough experience to spy effectively."

Jeho bit his lip mediatatively.

"So is Ahithopel after something specific – or was he just trailing a net in the river to see if it caught a fish?"

Caleb shrugged and shouted "Make way there!" to no more effect than usual.

ע

AYIN

The sixteenth letter of the Hebrew alphabet

I am your servant; give me discernment that I may understand your statutes.

Michal watched the departing figure of Jeho from behind an Egyptian screen in an upper room overlooking the courtyard. She beckoned to her handmaid and bodyguard and made her dignified way down the broad staircase, her silk gown sweeping out on either side with her attendants two steps behind her to right and left. One of Ahithopel's servants announced her, and Ahithopel rose and bowed as she floated imperiously into his reception room.

"Lady, excuse my keeping you waiting. You will understand that the king's humble servant has claims on his time which cannot be denied."

It crossed Michal's mind that one advantage of seeing Ahithopel was that no-one would suspect her of being physically attracted to the pinched-faced, wizened counsellor. Whatever the secret of his success might be, it was nothing to do with physical charm.

To be kept waiting had annoyed her sufficiently for her to register a protest with her host, of whose humility she was not convinced.

"I must say that there are several aspects to your invitation that I find extraordinary. For one thing, it might be considered more appropriate for you to wait on me if any meeting is to take place. Especially as your duties bring you to the palace on a daily basis.

For another thing, I am not accustomed to being kept waiting for anyone's sake."

This was not quite true, but she felt it would sound impressive enough for this courtier. She continued, "I saw Jehoshaphat the recorder leaving your house. I should have thought that I was at least as important as my lord the king's note-taker."

"Jehoshaphat has indeed been here, on business concerning the ambassadors from Tyre. He is the king's servant, as I am, and only the king's business could force me to keep you waiting, honoured lady. May I offer you some wine?"

"Thank you, I shall take none." She thought that she had shown her teeth sufficiently for this occasion. Unless she stormed out and left, it was time to conciliate the man, or at least find out what the business was about.

"I have some idea, Ahithopel, of the value of your services to the king. Your services are a source of honour for your name. So far as lies in my poor power, I am willing to support you and others in strengthening the kingdom and its authority. However, it is not clear to me what I could accomplish to this end."

"Lady, you are the queen of Israel."

His voice was deeply serious and still: it carried conviction.

"No-one but you calls me the queen. But I am the daughter of a king and I am the wife of a king. I have had to watch as my father's house has been consumed by the long war."

"Israel and Judah hold together now, just so."

He held his fists against each other, and jerked them apart.

"How easily they might come apart. The king is holding the kingdom together. For now. He can hold it together - because he won the war."

"Fighting the Philistines is one thing. Hebrews fighting Hebrews is another matter."

Michal looked troubled, as if saying the words might be enough to cause war to break out.

"Perhaps." Ahithopel's voice took on intensity. "It could happen - very easily. It would only take some busybody in the north, someone with enough hangers-on and parasites, someone who fancies himself a leader - to blow a trumpet. He'd shout curses on David and Judah and rule from Jerusalem and tell the Israelites they'd be better off without David. Oh, it could happen. But I shall do my best to see it doesn't."

"Is that why you go to so much trouble? Because you think Israel needs a king?"

"Yes, now it does. At one time we could manage without a king, just ruled by priests and judges and the law, but now we need a focus for our loyalty: we need someone to ride into Jerusalem on a white horse, someone to lead the army where it doesn't want to go, someone whose name will be on their lips when they climb the walls of enemy cities."

"David is a victorious king, of course."

"And that, lady Michal, is the vital thing. As you understand very well, so long as the king defeats his enemies the people will be behind him. But they won't send their sons off to be on impaled on Philistine spears if at the same time they are losing their sheep and goats and fields and olive trees. But if he fails - and every time fighting starts the potential for failure is there - then he will go down and a lot of people will go down with him."

It struck Michal that she would be among those to fall if the king fell. In the worst case, if a foreign army took Jerusalem, she would at best be dragged off through the burning ruins to some captain's harem, or more likely ravaged in her own home. She shuddered at the thought, and wondered about the thin-faced man opposite her.

Could he possibly survive the fall of David? If anyone could, he would.

She tried to get to the point.

"I understand that what you want, counsellor, is to keep the kingdom together. It is a noble goal. What I do not see is how I can be of any use to you in this undertaking."

Ahithopel picked up his staff and planted its end firmly on the floor: both his hands rested on its top.

"If I support the king's family I support the king, my lady."

"That's prettily said, counsellor, but what does it mean in fact? I can't influence the nobles of Israel not to break away from Judah, can I?"

"On that point, lady, I am not so certain. It may be that some people – both nobles and commoners in the north – might be more encouraged in their allegiance to the house of David."

"How?"

"It needn't take much effort on your part, my lady. You could cultivate people in the north. For example, if there are times when noblemen from the north come to Jerusalem, you could invite their wives to the palace."

"If I could put up with their manners I might. Some of them are probably reasonable company. So you think something as simple as inviting a fat northern matron for a bowl of wine might help to keep the kingdom together?"

"Little things count if they fall in the right place, lady." Ahithopel held out his staff in his right hand and tapped it in two spots on the floor in front of him.

"When the fat matron goes home she'll want everyone to know how gracious you were to her – that will be another village where you are called the queen, at least."

"Thank you for your advice, Ahithopel. I shall reflect on what you have said."

She stood to leave: Ahithopel stood to see her to the door, calling for servants to escort her. She gave him the tightest of smiles and left.

צ

TSADHE

The eighteenth letter of the Hebrew alphabet

Your statutes are for ever right; give me understanding that I may live.

Marion had set aside a room for the questioning of her servants: it was on the ground floor and, Jeho thought, was probably used as a bedchamber, although any sign of bedding had been removed in accordance with the solemnity of the occasion.

The first man he was to interview was a cook and butler, an Israelite of the tribe of Naphtali. He looked as if he his expertise in food and wine resulted from a good deal of practical experience.

"Name?"

"Orman."

"Do you know why you are here?"

"No idea, sir." That was a lie at least, but not a very serious one.

"What are your duties, Orman?"

The man shifted his weight uneasily from one foot to the other, and directed his answer to a tapestry over Jeho's head.

"I work in the kitchen mostly. Sometimes I wait on table when the master is entertaining."

"Do you know much of what goes on in the house - I mean the master's and the mistress' business?"

The man raised his eyebrows and almost grunted his reply, apparently surprised at his bringing the mistress into the conversation.

"Little enough. Of course they tell the butler how many are eating, and he tells us."

"Do you know that your mistress's sister Zilpah is betrothed to Shimron?"

The cook looked at Jeho as if he were not altogether right in the head.

"Of course I know that. The betrothal celebration lasted three days, and I did most of the cooking. And as for the wine that was drunk..."

His expression suggested both resentment of the work involved and admiration for some heroic drinking.

Jeho decided to get to the heart of the matter quickly.

"Have you heard any rumours about Shimron having an affair with a married woman?"

Orman still seemed to be concentrating intently on the tapestry.

"No , sir. As far as I know Shimron is an honest man."

"Are you sure?"

If anything, Orman's face was even more expressionless. "As I say, sir, all I know is that Shimron is betrothed to Zilpah."

Jeho dismissed him and discussed his testimony with Marion.

"At least Orman isn't a threat any more. He's told me he knows nothing. If he changes his story now he'll be discredited. Why did you suspect Orman?"

"Rebecca told me so. Do you want to speak to Rebecca?"

"Bring her in, please."

Jehoshaphat concentrated hard on the woman who entered the room in the unobtrusive manner of a personal servant. She stood in front of him with her hands loosely clasped in front of her waist, head slightly bowed, and looked at him, obviously waiting for him to speak.

"Name?"

"Rebecca, servant to the lady of Shimron, master of this house."

"How long have you been in her service?"

"Two years, sir."

She was obviously not going to give away much unsolicited information, but Jehoshaphat was accustomed to that.

"Do you know that your mistress's sister Zilpah is betrothed?"

Rebecca's surprise at the question was genuine.

"Of course I know that. She and Shimron often visit this house."

"Do you believe that Zilpah and Shimron are faithful to each other?"

She tossed her head and gave a little snort. "I'm sure it's none of my business."

"Very discreet of you. But don't tell me that the servants in this house never talk to each other about the mistress's family."

That brought a faint smile.

"Of course there's gossip. But I think they're as happy as any other betrothed couple. Of course, Shimron's a man – and not the ugliest one I've ever seen."

She shot a complicit little look at Jeho, who was shocked at her boldness. Did she not realize how serious this was? Jeho asked her the same question he had asked Orman.

"Have you heard any rumours about Shimron having an affair with a married woman?"

"No sir."

"Do not lie to me."

She looked abashed, and hesitated a moment.

"I don't wish to speak of such wickedness, I mean. There's no truth in such wicked stories. If I heard anything like that I should just tell them to shut up."

"Really. What about the plot?"

"I don't know of any plot, sir."

"I think you know very well what I mean. The plot to discredit your mistress, to get Shimron put to death and to deliver his vineyard into Ahithopel's hands."

Her head was bowed, face firmly towards the floor.

"I know nothing of any such plot, sir. It's far above me, all the doings of great men like Ahithopel and yourself."

"I think you knew all about this story of a plot. I think you passed on the details."

She kept her head bowed: her shoulders trembling.

"Who told you that the servants were in Ahithopel's plot? Or did the story originate with you, Rebecca?"

She flashed a glance at him, and immediately lowered her head again.

"It did not, sir. That was what was commonly said - in the kitchens."

"So you did know. Who exactly told you, Rebecca?"

"I don't remember, sir. It could have been Orman, or one of the others."

Jeho dismissed her with a wave. You could tell a lot about someone from the servants with whom she surrounded herself. There was a subtlety about this servant that bore witness to at least equal subtlety in the mistress.

There was a bustle at the door and Marion entered, dismissing her servant. She waited for a couple of seconds and re-opened the door, but no-one was behind it. She closed it again and sat down elegantly in a large wooden chair inlaid with ivory decoration, her bold eyes scanning Jeho's face.

"Have you found anything from your queries?"

"Not a great deal directly. But I have started to form some ideas. I must say that I didn't entirely believe Rebecca. I wouldn't trust her, if I were in your position. I don't think she was telling me the truth."

"Why would she lie?"

"It could be a private grudge. She could just have something against the other servants, and be trying to get them into trouble with you."

Marion nodded enthusiastically. "I've always thought Rebecca was a deep one. She could very well be playing some such game. There's something I want to show you – come with me."

Marion led him to the less public rooms at the back of the house, an area usually not to be shown to a distinguished guest.

"This room is where the female servants sleep." Jeho had already worked that out for himself. "And this bundle is Rebecca's."

She felt inside the bundle of clothing and frowned, then opened it out. Clearly whatever she was looking for was missing.

"What was it you found?" asked Jeho, thinking that Marion obviously regarded nothing to do with her servants as outside her purview.

"She had a little leather pouch with three silver coins in it. I couldn't understand where she could have got them."

"She might have decided they weren't well enough hidden here," said Jeho trying not to sound sarcastic. "Or they might have been stolen. But at any rate, you think she has received a payment from someone outside your household to betray you, am I right?"

"That's exactly what I think."

"Obviously you haven't challenged her about this."

"No. I don't want to put her on her guard."

Looking back at the interview with her, Jeho thought that Rebecca was already quite wary enough, as well she might be with a mistress like Marion. It should be remembered, he thought, that Marion was in fear of her life. Or was she, really? Little in her controlled manner suggested it.

Deborah had been interested in Marion and Shimron ever since she had first heard of them. Jeho had wondered if she was jealous of Marion for approaching him and taking up so much of his time, but he later decided that she was just interested in the situation itself. Certainly it had all the elements needed to interest anyone, with its possibilities of adultery, corruption and injustice. That evening Deborah was keen to hear the details of the interviews. Jeho added his thoughts about the reliability of the servants he had interviewed.

"It's certain that Rebecca is not telling us anything like as much as she could."

"Do you think she's in Ahithopel's pay?"

"Probably. But she's taking a tremendous risk if she is. She could just disappear, I suppose."

"Yes. Perhaps it's not so hard to leave everything behind when you don't have much to start with. But not alone, I think. Anyway, if she were trying to get someone accused of adultery – falsely – what would be the penalty for that?"

Jeho pursed his lips as he thought for a moment.

"If she formally brought an accusation, knowing it to be ungrounded, to destroy someone's life – that would be false testimony. The sentence would be death."

Deborah grimaced at the thought of a stoning.

"Who would take that risk?"

"Someone very bold might, if someone powerful had promised to protect her - and she believed him."

It was time for Jeho to find out a little more about Rebecca, and that meant some work for Caleb. Although fading into the background was not a trait one would have associated with him, he could manage to gather a surprising amount of information about people without arousing suspicion. Jeho gave him Rebecca's description and told him to follow her from Marion's house and find out what he could. Caleb was obviously pleased with the job. He lifted the hood of his cloak over his head and slipped out. Jeho hoped he didn't overdo the secretiveness and get himself arrested. Deborah was already relaxing on the roof with a flask of wine: he followed her up.

ל

LAMED

The twelfth letter of the Hebrew alphabet

The wicked are waiting to destroy me, but I will ponder your statutes.

They had started on the second flask when a commotion broke out downstairs. Deborah's maid sprang down and they heard a sharp laugh. She had regained her composure by the time she returned with Caleb. He was in a bad shape. He was going to have a very black eye in the near future, and his nose had obviously been bleeding.

"I see Rebecca got rough with you, Caleb."

"I don't know who it was, master, but it wasn't Rebecca. Someone much bigger and stronger, but that's all I know."

"Start from when you left Marion's house."

"Rebecca came out on her own, well wrapped in a cloak with a hood. She went around the neighbouring streets in a circle to start with, then towards the palace. I was following her at a distance, carefully because she kept looking round."

"So she knew or suspected that she was being followed."

"I don't think she saw me, but she was certainly being cautious from the moment she left the house."

"Then what?"

"She went into a little side street. I followed her down it but as soon as I turned the corner some one hit me, hard. When I woke up there was no-one there."

Jeho could see no chance of finding out anything else that night. He thought that Caleb would be keen to play the part of the put-upon servant suffering all kinds of indignities for his master. It was as well to let him get on with it, with Deborah's maidservant. Deborah ordered her to see to Caleb's wounds and they could hear giggling from the kitchen as they settled back with the flask of wine.

The next day Michal followed up Ahithopel's proposal by entertaining a visitor who had a rich store of anecdotes.

"So you see, lady, when it came to the time to use the barley, it turned out that there was only a layer of barley in each of the sacks – about half a cubit – and the rest sand and rubbish."

"Really? How wicked of them. But did your husband's men not notice anything when they moved the sacks? The weight must have been wrong."

"Indeed it was, lady Michal. But the wicked fellow had used his own men to move the sacks into our barn, pretending he was doing us a service. That's why I never trust any Gadites, my lady."

"I can see why you would find it hard to do so."

Michal was enjoying the conversation more than she had expected. The first recipient of her new generosity to the northerners was a pleasantly plump woman a little older than herself, the wife of a clan chief from Megiddo. At first she had been quiet, a little overcome to find herself not only in the palace but in Michal's private apartment, but now she had lost her reserve and it was impossible to restrain her chatter.

Ahithopel had sent a message about the forthcoming visit of her husband and suggested that the wife might appreciate some attention from Michal: the maidservant she had sent to invite the woman had found it hard to convince her that it wasn't a hoax. At any event, Michal was doing her patriotic duty to strengthen the kingdom.

"Tell me about your children, Helah."

"I have only one son, lady Michal. His name is Eliath, a fine boy, seven years old. I wish I could have had more, of course ..."

48

She tailed off as her awkwardness returned. It was a difficult subject for Michal, but she pursued it.

"Is he like his father?"

"More like me, lady Michal, but his father won't hear that."

They smiled at the obtuseness of men. Her confidence returning, Helah leaned forward and whispered.

"I had tried so long to give him a child, but I was barren for years. I think he would have divorced me if it hadn't been for my portion."

"So it ended well, at any rate. You must be very thankful to the Everlasting that you had a fine boy."

Helah looked confused and a little guilty. Michal could guess why. The visit was soon over.

In another part of the palace, Caleb was telling Jeho that the King's messenger was asking about the order of business for the day.

"Tell the king's servant there's only one case today, but it's a murder."

Caleb scuttled away with the message: Jeho reflected on the case. It had come to the king because the victim's widow could get no justice in her town of Mizpeh. The perpetrators were too well connected. If the verdict was guilty then the sentence would be death. Jeho would try to make sure that the king ordered sentence to be carried out in Mizpeh rather than in Jerusalem. It was not enough for the murderer to die: he should be humbled in front of his family and friends as well.

If the verdict went the other way, then the widow was in danger herself. She could face the punishment for false witness, in a trial for life. She was taking an enormous risk.

The woman who was ushered into the king's presence was short and stout: she carried herself with dignity. Her face was rigid and strained, but Jeho thought from the lines on it that she was more accustomed to laughter than tears.

The two men standing opposite her were two of the elders of Mizpeh. They looked defiant but nervous, as if they were trying to combine respect for the court with contempt for the widow.

"Is your name Tamar, widow of Shama?"

"It is so, my lord."

"What is your charge?"

"I accuse Helez and Zelek of the murder of my husband Shama."

"How do you answer, Helez and Zelek?"

They denied the charge vehemently.

"Tamar, state your case."

"My husband was a merchant who bought and sold linen and other cloths, as well as spices. He set out for Egypt with a large sum of money in gold and silver."

"Was it known he was travelling with money?"

What a pointless question, Jeho thought. The widow scarcely concealed her impatience:

"Of course everyone knew what he was doing. He had no reason to keep it secret. He was planning to go overland to Joppa and take ship to Egypt from there."

"Did your husband and you come from Mizpeh?"

"No. We moved there when our house in Beersheba was burned down in the fighting."

Jeho was glad that that point had come to light. Recent incomers were ranged against town elders, connected to almost all their neighbours by marriage or blood. That explained how the elders had thought they could get away with the crime.

"How did you know that he had stolen your husband's money?"

"I recognised one of the coins. The hole in the middle had been punched twice, done in a clumsy way. I recognised because my husband tried to give it me once and I said I wanted a perfect one." She was close to tears now.

The king spoke: "Show me your money."

The accused man beckoned reluctantly to a servant who produced a money-bag from his clothing. He emptied it over the table in front of the king, and shook it out. None of the coins corresponded to Tamar's description.

Jeho's eyes ran around the room and he saw something that made him look twice: a row of coins adorning the serving girl standing behind Zelek. Was it she who had flinched when the coins were mentioned? He called her forward, and fingered her necklace.

"Where did you get this?"

Her voice was low and trembling: "My master gave it to me."

Shouting broke out. Zelek was impassive. When order was restored, it was a simple matter to break him down: his main concern appeared to be to take Helez down with him.

Over dinner that evening Jeho told Deborah about the case. He asked her, "How can people want money so much?"

Deborah pursed her lips.

"Perhaps we're rich enough not to see money as a problem. I think some of the reason is because people are afraid of what tomorrow may bring. Money can help with a lot of misfortunes. Suppose all your cattle die – a rich man can go out and buy more: a poor one can't."

Jeho was unimpressed.

"Money can't buy you health."

"True. But a sick rich man is still more comfortable than a sick poor one. And I think that's why we all value money – in all its forms; land, cattle, horses, gold and silver. If we have it, we don't have to depend on the Almighty for our needs: we can meet them from our own pockets."

Jeho nodded in appreciation. His wife's depths were a constant surprise to him.

ז

ZAYIN

The seventh letter of the Hebrew alphabet

Your decrees are the theme of my song wherever I lodge.

Jeho liked his house to be a place of peace: his refuge from the palace to-and-fro of business and protocol. Tonight it was obviously not to be so: runners were arriving at regular intervals to give messages from captains and courtiers, or to ask for details of arrangements he had communicated to their masters a week previously.

"So I shall be on my own tonight as well?" Deborah was only pretending to be annoyed, Jeho decided. She understood that this was no ordinary occasion.

"I fear so. Try to remember that tomorrow will be the greatest day in the history of the kingdom. In fact, I think you could say the greatest day since we came into this land in Joshua's days. What is it, Caleb?"

"Will you go armed and armoured, master?"

"Not for the ride into the city. But bring a couple of daggers with you, just in case."

The king and most of the court were to ride out the evening before to escort the Ark into the city on the final leg of the journey.

Jeho stood for a moment, looking at the tent that stood silhouetted against the dying light of the western sky. It formed a link all the way back to Moses and his brother Aaron the first priest. Without a doubt not one piece of cloth remained from those days, but the tradition was continuous nonetheless. And from now, it would all be different. For good or ill, until the end of days Jerusalem would be the only place where any Hebrew would build a temple to the glory of the Everlasting.

Samuel had not lived to see this day, but his hands had anointed David as king. The king was a link to Samuel, the most notable priest since Aaron himself. Samuel, dedicated to the service of the Lord from before his birth, whom the Lord had called as a child to serve him, the one who had consecrated the only two kings in Israel's history. Jeho recalled the story of how Eli, Samuel's mentor, had taken calmly the news of his sons' deaths, but the capture of this very ark had killed him. Now the king Samuel had anointed was about to install that same ark as the focal point of the worship of the nation.

Soon after daybreak, the courtiers and senior officers assembled before the tent containing the Ark. The king led the prayers for the people and the city of Jerusalem. Then the Levites entered the tent and after a few moments emerged, poles on their shoulders. In the middle was the Ark itself, the most striking object Jeho had ever seen. It was surmounted by the figures of two angels facing each other. In the sudden hush when the Ark came out into the daylight, sun gleaming on gold, he could almost hear the voices of the angels themselves.

The king shouted "Rejoice!" and a wave of shouting broke over the assembly.

The sun was well up before they were under way.

All were on foot, except a troop of cavalry Joab had insisted on stationing at the rear of the procession. They were there to react quickly to any attempted raid to capture or damage the Ark. For the same reason, there were archers unobtrusively positioned on the walls.

There was a pause at the city gates before the moment of entry.

A shofar's high and urgent note set every nerve on edge. A thrill went through him as the Levites entered through the gates and every throat cheered.

Once they were in the city everything seemed much wilder and more concentrated. People were everywhere, hanging over parapets on rooftops, cheering out of windows, pushing up against the soldiers who maintained a cordon around the priests carrying the Ark. Some beat on tambourines or drums, some blew horns, all of them cheered and shouted.

In front of the Ark went David himself, dancing enthusiastically and jumping from foot to foot. The Levites crashed their cymbals: the sound of the harps and lyres that Jeho could see in front of him was lost in the general rejoicing. But he joined with them in the song of celebration.

"Let the heavens rejoice, let the earth be glad; let them say among the nations 'The Lord reigns!'

Let the sea resound, and all that is in it; let the fields rejoice, and all in them!"

They passed the palace on the way to the area where the tent stood. The music stopped for the burnt offerings and the peace offerings.

Everyone got a loaf, as well as a date-cake and a raisin-cake. Just the preparation of those gifts had been a significant logistical exercise. But Jeho felt proud in his heart that no citizen would be going to bed that night hungry: no family was prevented from joining in the rejoicing because a child was starving.

He caught sight of Deborah: he tingled with joy as her eyes met his. She was surrounded by their servants, all swept up against a wall by the press of the crowd. He forced his way over to them and shouted above the noise.

"The Ark is here at last!"

He could see in her eyes that she understood.

"This is where it belongs for ever!"

Michal had taken up position at her window in the palace to watch the procession. She felt distanced from the celebration in the street: the prancing mob disgusted her. She had allowed her maidservant to leave the palace and attend the celebration: she saw her clearly clapping and dancing.

Then she caught sight of the king her husband. She thought king David himself was no more dignified than her maidservant. After the celebrations she went to find David to tell him so.

"How the king of Israel made an exhibition of himself: showing his legs and more in front of servant girls like a vulgar buffoon!"

"I will celebrate before the Lord, Michal. I am ruler over Israel by the Lord's appointment: not your father, or anyone from his family. And those servant girls you speak of will honour me, not Saul or anyone else. And I celebrate the Lord even more than this, and will become even more undignified."

She saw his anger, and she saw the love behind it. Her posing and airs were suddenly so many dirty rags in her sight. She moved toward him, and laid her hand on his arm. His face softened.

"O Michal, how much I have loved you. You are the wife of my youth, the first woman I ever loved. Do you remember how you saved me when your father sent his men for my head? How they found a dummy with a goatskin wig?"

She smiled at the memory, and held his hand to her cheek.

"My father never cared for me, and he never consulted my wishes. He gave me to you – I was well pleased at that, believe me – but he thought I was still his to give afterwards. That was the worst moment of my life, David."

His arms enfolded her.

Jeho and Deborah finally got home to a house buzzing with excitement. There was music and dancing in the street outside and generous quantities of wine being shared inside the house. They were just about to relax on the couch for a rest before dinner when Deborah was called to the door. When she returned her face was wreathed in smiles.

"We have a special treat tonight. It's a present from Joab: a big fish; a turbot."

"I wonder why Joab would send me a present. Very good of him of course."

"The messenger just said it was a token of the general's esteem."

"I must be doing something right if Joab has so much esteem for me. Or perhaps he just doesn't like fish."

"It was already gutted and stuffed with olives, so I just ordered it to be baked and sent in."

"Excellent. I hope it won't be long."

Caleb carried the fish in on a platter. Jeho and Deborah took their places. He leaned forward and pulled of a piece of the glistening flesh. As it came away he caught a glimpse of something earth-coloured inside the fish. Whatever it was, it seemed not to be stuffing. He took a grip of the object and pulled it out, scattering fragments of fish over the table.

"Whatever that is it isn't an olive - no, it's a potsherd," said Deborah. "Look, there's something written on this side."

Jeho cleaned off the fish from the potsherd and read "Orman lies. Meet me fourth hour tonight at Dung Gate alone."

"Do you know, Jeho, I suddenly don't feel very hungry."

He leaned back from the table, with a frown on his features. "Why did you think the fish came from Joab?"

"The man who brought it said it was from him. Of course, that proves nothing."

"We mustn't accept any more gifts of food or drink without proof of the identity of the giver. This could just as easily have been poison as a message."

"Are you going to this rendezvous, Jeho?"

He looked her in the eyes and inclined his head slightly. "I have to find out more about this."

"I wish you wouldn't go, Jeho."

Deborah was serious but knew that there was no turning her husband aside when he was this determined.

"I am going."

"Take Caleb with you at least."

"I shall be safe. I'm not going there looking for trouble: at the first sign of anything wrong I'll be gone. But I have to go alone. If I frighten off my informer I won't learn anything."

She needed some reassurance, thought Jeho. He had no intention of getting hurt. He thought about taking a weapon but decided against it.

Shortly before the hour Jeho put on a dark cloak with a hood. He slipped as quietly as possible through the still streets, where only the muffled sound of laughter from wineshops broke the quiet. A drunk staggered up to him and clung on to him with his arms round Jeho's neck. Jeho pushed him off in disgust and he crashed against a wall. Jeho heard the sound of noisy retching behind him.

It was not far to the gate, and he was resigned to a lengthy wait.

Jeho heard a low whistle and simultaneously heard a sound of smashing pottery and Caleb's voice shouting a warning. He threw himself full length and over his head heard the whoosh of an arrow. Then he heard Caleb shouting and the sound of running feet. He got up and ran after the shouts.

Caleb was standing on a corner, having lost his quarry.

"I thought I told you to stay at home!"

"My lady Deborah countermanded your orders, master."

"What's all this commotion?" A guard had descended from the gatehouse.

Jeho had taken the precaution of bringing with him his seal of office, and fortunately the guard was sober enough to recognise it. "I was attacked - look, you can see the arrow there. But he got away."

The guard examined the arrow closely, but there was nothing useful to be gleaned from it.

"I can offer you an escort home, sir."

"Thank you, I have my servant now and I don't think he'll try again tonight. Good night, watchman."

"Good night, sir."

Caleb was examining the potsherds on the ground, and glanced up at the building from which it had fallen.

"We know there were two of them at least, master. One to drop the pot when he heard the whistle, and the bowman at ground level."

"What was the idea? The pot kills me or if it doesn't the arrow does?"

"No, master, the pot was to make you look up. Then the bowman gets a clear shot at your throat. The throat's the most certain way of killing a man by bowshot."

"I won't ask how you know. So they meant to kill me?"

"No doubt of it."

It was difficult for Jeho to reprimand Deborah as she deserved for sending Caleb after him. The image of himself lying in the gate with an arrow in his throat was a hard one to shake off.

ה

HE

The fifth letter of the Hebrew alphabet

Direct me in the path of your commands, for there I find delight.

"Anything else, Jehoshaphat?" The king looked as if he rather hoped there would not be anything else: he was itching to get out of the palace and on horseback again. Jehoshaphat decided there was only one item that needed to be mentioned without more delay.

"You may have heard that there is a report from Jericho, my lord. Nahash, king of the Ammonites, has died. He had been ill for some time, as we knew."

The king nodded.

"So I heard from Ahithopel. I am sorry for it. He was good to me when I couldn't be of any help to him."

A thought must have struck him suddenly, as he frowned and asked, "Will there be any unrest? Is Hanun well established?"

"Yes, my lord. As much as one can expect at this stage. Nobody else is expected to make any sort of challenge, at least not unless something unexpected happens."

"I think we should be seen to support him. That will help to cement him on the throne. I'll send a mission to express sympathy for his father's death."

He stared down at the table for a few seconds, before he looked up and smiled at the recorder.

"I want you to go, Jehoshaphat. This calls for judgement and you have that. I want Eleazar to go as well."

Jehoshaphat understood that Eleazar would be there as an unmistakable reminder that there were more like him in the army.

The king sprang vigorously out of his chair and set off with an almost undignified haste. Jehoshaphat hoped that he would be as enthusiastic about riding through the Judean hills when he reached the king's age, but he rather doubted it.

Whom do I have to inform first, then, he wondered to himself. Obviously Eleazar, and Seraiah the secretary to take over my duties here, and I must get a message to Jericho to prepare our accommodation there ... but no question who was the first priority.

Deborah was not delighted at her husband's mission to the east, but she was equally obviously trying to remind herself what an honour it was for her husband to be the King's ambassador.

"How long will you be there, then, three days? You'll need four fine linen garments at least, and something for riding... how many servants are going? Well then, when do you expect to decide? And don't let Eleazar treat you as if it's a military campaign, none of that riding after sunset, you've got your dignity to consider..."

It was agreed on all sides that Caleb would accompany the two principals and see to their daily needs. Eleazar, being a true soldier, made it known that he did not really need a servant for such a short expedition, but indicated that he would be happy to let Caleb wait on him as well.

They clearly needed gifts for the new king. Jeho decided to propose to the king that they offer a pair of horses of the finest quality. They would have the advantage as gifts that they could carry themselves to Rabbeh. He thought of asking for an escort, but decided that any party that included Eleazar was unlikely to be attacked on the way.

So when they set out Caleb was riding one horse and leading another, as was Eleazar. The road descended steeply into the

Jordan valley, and they were in particular hurry. It was better to take their time and avoid accidents, in particular to their riderless horses intended as gifts.

Jericho was their last Jewish city of any size before they crossed into the territory of the Ammonites. It was a strangely undefended city for one lying so close to the borders of Judah. They stayed as guests with the captain who was responsible for calling out the levy in the Jericho area. As the local military commander Joseph was well informed about events in Ammon: Jehoshaphat was well aware that he was the source of much of the news about the Ammonites that came to the court through official channels. It was well worth sounding him out about the state of affairs in Ammon.

Jehoshaphat soon revised his initial view that the commander was unfriendly to them. He decided that he was a man who had little small talk but who could be voluble on subjects he knew something about.

Over the dinner table that evening Jehoshaphat asked Joseph whether the new king was secure in power. Joseph put down his roast kid thigh and stared at it thoughtfully.

"Our information comes principally from merchants travelling through who have been in Rabbeh. Some are more reliable than others of course, and some may have reasons of their own for what they say. But there seem to be two factions at court: basically a younger element attached to Hanun and an older element from his father's day."

Joseph's eyes had a hooded, heavy-lidded appearance: Jeho decided that this was why he had thought the man forbidding at first.

Eleazar asked "Aren't the Ammonites related to us in some way?"

"They are — but it wouldn't be very tactful to dwell on it too much. Do you remember the tale of Lot and his two daughters?"

Eleazar's face lit up with a salacious grin.

"Ah yes. The ones who got their father drunk to solve the husband shortage. So that's where the Ammonites come from."

"Quite. Lot's children and grandchildren at one and the same time. So I don't intend to bring up too much ancient history, not on a diplomatic mission."

"I can see that. How do you plan to take it? You're the courtier: I'm just a soldier: I'll follow your lead – once we're there."

"I think the best approach is to emphasise the personal aspect of David's relations with Nahash, and to make it clear that we seen Hanun as building on the foundations of his father's works. I don't think there's much opportunity to discuss business yet: let Hanun find his feet first."

"All that sort of thing's your department. I just want to get us there and back in one piece."

The next morning Jeho found that he missed Deborah more than he would have expected. He was accustomed to travelling to nearby countries on diplomatic missions, and normally he was so occupied with the activities of the mission that he had little time to moon over being away from home – and, if truth were told, he enjoyed the finery, feasting and ceremony that were a part of such trips. On this occasion, however, he missed her, and not just, he felt, because they were living relatively simply. He would be glad to be home after this mission.

The steep uphill road was so hard on the horses that the envoys dismounted in places, making their way on foot up the eastern side of the valley. It was impossible to make progress on that road in the heat of the afternoon.

In the early evening Eleazar noticed carrion birds gathering by the road ahead. He had Jeho and Caleb dismount and wait while he scouted, but soon he waved them up to join him. They examined the corpse he had found lying by the side of the road. The man had died of an arrow wound. The broken-off arrowhead was behind his right ear.

"How do you think he died?" Jeho said.

"I don't think it was suicide," offered Caleb.

"Quiet, Caleb. What do you think, Eleazar?"

"Bandits. You find them sometimes on this road - or rather they find you."

They buried the corpse perfunctorily and continued.

At the border they stated their business to a bored-looking officer in charge of the sentry detail. Whatever changes the new king was likely to bring about would make little difference out there, or at least that seemed to be the attitude. This was their first opportunity to speak to Ammonites, and they found, as they had been led to expect, that the language was sufficiently like Hebrew for them to understand and make themselves understood. The officer detached one of his men to keep them company as far as the next garrisoned town, with strict orders to return as soon as possible after handing them on. Jehoshaphat wondered whether desertion was a problem for them.

It made sense for Jeho and Eleazar to take the opportunity of the journey to get to know each other better. Over their evening meal, Jeho asked, "Who is your hero, Eleazar?"

"That's easy, Jeho. The leader I most admire is Joshua."

"Why him? Of course, he was a great leader ..."

Eleazar swallowed off a cup of wine.

"He was the greatest general who ever led the Hebrews. He chose the right point of attack, crossing the Jordan with his rear area secure. He took the major city - Jericho - on his line of advance, decisively, and then he extended his area of control into the hill country. It was the most magnificent feat of arms in our history, and it made us what we are."

It was clear to Jeho that Eleazar had given the matter some thought. He was not surprised that Eleazar, asked about his hero, had come up with a military leader.

Eleazar popped a dried fig into his mouth and chewed it before continuing. "Tell me about your hero, Jeho."

"My hero - there are so many - but I think Joseph."

"Joseph? That's an interesting choice."

"He followed the truth and the truth led him through slavery and prison to being the saviour of his people."

"He might have followed the truth for himself but he didn't always spread it to others, did he? He deceived his own brothers about his identity."

"True."

Jeho had to accept that Eleazar had made a good point.

"That's not the aspect I was thinking about, of course. I was thinking about the truth he had revealed to him in his dreams, how he told the truth to Pharaoh, how Potiphar's wife lied about him, how his brothers lied to their father about his death in the wilderness."

"Are there never any good lies, Jeho? Think of Joshua again, about Rahab and the spies. She lied to the soldiers who came looking for the spies. Wasn't she right to do that?"

"Usually people who lie bring shame on themselves. Like Abraham, pretending Sarah was his sister."

"Don't you ever lie on your diplomatic business?"

"In fact I don't think I have ever lied on diplomatic business. Of course one doesn't tell everything one knows: there are weaknesses that on doesn't want to reveal sometimes. But saying something that isn't true, knowing it to be untrue is very dangerous for a diplomat, I think. If the lie comes to light – and they generally do sooner or later – what credibility does he have?"

"You still haven't answered me about Rahab."

Jeho smiled.

"That's right, I didn't. I'm not really sure. I just pray not to be in the same position myself."

Eleazar grinned at him and took the last fig. "You don't deserve this if you can't come down on one side or the other."

"At least there's one consolation: we won't have to lie on this mission. It's just a straightforward message of condolences and paying respects to the new king."

Jeho had always thought of Eleazar as a straightforward character, a bluff and capable soldier. He was starting to see unsuspected depths in him. Perhaps Eleazar now trusted him enough to reveal another side.

כ

KAPH

The eleventh letter of the Hebrew alphabet

The arrogant dig pitfalls for me, contrary to your law.

The road snaked round a last corner and they had their first sight of Rabbeh. The great city of the Ammonites dominated the plain spread out to the south, from a citadel surrounded by casemate walls obviously designed to allow the citadel to hold out indefinitely if the civil area of the city were captured.

"Not so beautiful as Jerusalem," Jehoshaphat remarked in a low tone.

Eleazar kept his gaze fixed on the city as he shielded his eyes against the morning sun.

"Still impressive, though."

As they approached, the escort blew his horn at regular intervals, giving rise to a flurry of activity above the main gate.

Caleb, leading the horses, was in his turn led off by a groom. Inside the palace they were immediately cooler, not only shielded from the midday heat, but also fanned by patient slaves moving their arms with economic rhythmic swings. The spacious vestibule was hung with tapestries in bold patterns: in the centre of room were chairs of acacia wood which Jeho and Eleazar were invited to occupy. After a few minutes the palace chamberlain was announced, and they rose as he swept in followed by a couple of minor officials.

The chamberlain, whose name was Ebom, was a very fat man, whose expensively dyed robes hung like a canopy down from his middle. He probably had very fine shoes, thought Jeho, but his servants would see more of them than anyone else. His eyes glinted from the middle of a fleshy face fringed by an intricately barbered beard.

He welcomed them and told them that their audience with the king would take place the next morning. One of his junior officials was assigned to make them comfortable and, if they wished, to take them to visit the sights of the city.

After their feet had been ceremonially washed and they had had time to examine their comfortable chamber, Jeho and Eleazar were ready to accept the offer of a late afternoon stroll around the notable buildings of Rabbeh. The first notable sight was of course the palace itself, with its tapestries, elaborate vases, silk hangings and other fine examples of craftsmen's work. They also saw the royal armouries with bronze and iron swords, shields, spears and even some siege equipment.

On the way out of the palace they stopped to look at a guard detail turning away a man who had asked for an audience with the king. He was obviously emotional, and kept shouting, "Justice, justice from Hanun". The guards finally thrust him down the steps with the butt end of their spears.

"Does Hanun not admit his subjects before him to present their petitions?" Jeho asked their escort.

"The admission of supplicants to the presence of the king is managed by the officials of the court, of course. It is a heavy responsibility. Clearly they inform themselves about the nature of the petition and the nature of the petitioner. It must be the same at King David's court, I imagine."

Neither he nor they mentioned bribery, but it hung unspoken in the air.

"The practices of my lord's court differ to some degree, I think."

It was too insulting to leave it at that.

"Perhaps Hanun will institute changes in the kingdom?"

"You may be assured of that, my lord Jehoshaphat."

An uneasy silence followed this exchange. The city was stirring again after its afternoon repose, and a good many people thronged the streets. Several of the citizens stared at them curiously, but they felt insulated from contact with the Ammonites by the presence of the official and his slaves. An urchin who ran up asking for money got a slap on the side of the head from one of the retinue, and slunk away howling.

The temple of Moloch was unmistakable: as soon as Jeho saw it he knew what it must be and could hardly believe that he had recognised it from outside the city walls. It rose higher than the royal palace and the whole facade gave off waves of heat reflected from black polished stone.

The temple of Moloch hammered Jeho's senses. The first impression was of sheer size. The great statue of the god dominated the dark interior, glowering down with an expression of contempt and spite. Jeho guessed that the darkness of the temple was meant to emphasise the fires lit within the idol for sacrifice. The scent of incense was mingled with other, darker, smells that rose into his brain from octaves deeper. He gazed with horrified fascination at the metal forearms of the god, crossed before its chest. When the worshippers were at their most frenzied, with cymbals crashing and priests cutting themselves with knives, when the fires were banked high, that was the spot where infant lives were sacrificed to Moloch. That was where fathers would place their children and watch their small bodies bake in the god's arms.

Jeho felt sick, disgusted and guilty for even witnessing the spot where the sacrifices took place. He pulled Eleazar's sleeve.

"I have to get out, now."

Eleazar turned in silence and their guide followed them out, having made an obeisance before the god.

The slaves had waited for them outside the temple. Jeho was aware of their curiosity at his whitened face and strained eyes, but they would never of course give tongue to it.

Their escort did his best to hide his contempt on the way back to the palace, where he suggested that they might want to retire early before their audience the next day.

They did indeed go to bed soon after dusk, but although Eleazar appeared to fall asleep as soon as his head met the pillow Jeho had an uneasy night. Whenever he closed his eyes the image of the idol of Moloch came to haunt him. He did not feel fully refreshed when the sun streaming in woke Eleazar.

Their audience was scheduled for mid-morning, so they had time for Jeho to practice his speech with Eleazar taking the king's role before they were summoned. The servants looked uneasy, as if such play-acting might be considered mockery of the king and merely witnessing it could make them culpable.

Jehoshaphat could not read Hanun's expression with any certainty. If he wasn't giving anything away, that was his way of proceeding. He knew what his message was in any case. He stepped forward and made a gentle obeisance.

"O King, Hanun, son of Nahash the departed, lord of Rabbeh and ruler of the Ammonites, I bear greetings from my lord David, son of Jesse, King of the children of Israel."

Hanun had inclined his head at the mention of his titles, but his face was still giving nothing away. Jehoshaphat continued, "The King your father, whose memory be for ever blessed, ruled in wisdom and peace and laid in his day the foundations for a lasting kingdom of peace and prosperity. His departure is a grievous loss to the children of Ammon and to the friends of Ammon, among whom my lord King David is pleased to be counted."

The chamberlain stepped forward between the King and the envoy, slightly too quickly for court protocol, thought Jehoshaphat.

"The King has heard the words of King David. It is the wish of my Lord the King now to consult with his council as to the proper reply to make to those words. If you please to withdraw, you may refresh yourselves at your leisure."

He beckoned an obviously minor official who bowed in the direction of the King and led off Eleazar and Jehoshaphat. They both made their bows and followed. Jehoshaphat caught

Eleazar's eye and tried to put as strong a hint of silence into the glance as he could.

The room to which they were led contained comfortable couches and respectable wooden chairs: on a low table there was a bowl of grapes: a maidservant immediately appears with a tray on which there were two cups and a flask of wine, which she served to them. At least we aren't in prison yet, thought Jehoshaphat, who had detected a false note in their reception in the audience chamber. Of course, that could be what they're discussing now. When the maidservant had left he placed his mouth close to Eleazar's ear.

"I think there's something wrong here."

"We could easily escape from here. This window is set in an outside wall of the palace."

"We mustn't. That would be putting us in the wrong. Even if they kill us we have to let it happen, so that all the wrong is on their side."

"Ach!" Eleazar pushed him away in disgust and stalked angrily across the room.

The door was flung open. The chamberlain entered, his fat face distorted with spite. A squad of guards followed. Jehoshaphat was yanked to his feet roughly: two guards took hold of Eleazar's arms.

"The king has seen through your duplicity. He has seen you to be spies, and you will be expelled forthwith!"

The guards shoved them into the corridor and down a flight of steps.

As they approached the palace entry there was a blast of trumpets, and a herald cried, "People of Rabbeh, see how the King treats those who spy and plot against his throne!"

The midday sun beat down on their bare heads and rebounded from the broad shallow steps in front of the palace. Hundreds of mocking faces concentrated on the ambassadors who were roughly forced onto wooded chairs at the top of the steps. Rough hands tugged at their beards and inexpertly wielded shears.

Jehoshaphat realised that they were shaving only one side of his face as the laughter grew and grew. Then they were jerked to their feet, and the shears were turned on their clothes. The crowd grew almost delirious with laughter as the bottom half of Eleazar's robe was torn away to expose his nakedness. Then it was Jehoshaphat's turn.

A kick landed on Jehoshaphat's bare buttocks and forced him staggering down the steps. Some of the jeering mob aimed kicks at them, some made obscene gestures mocking circumcision. Jeho saw nothing clearly, just dirt and flying limbs as he stumbled around under blow after blow, on his head, back, buttocks and legs. They're going to kill us, he thought. Will they burn us alive in the temple, or just kick us to death? Then suddenly he was in the sun again. The final kicks sent them sprawling outside the city gates.

ש

SHIN

The twenty-first letter of the Hebrew alphabet

Rulers persecute me without cause, but my heart trembles at your word.

When they felt out of immediate danger from the city, they stopped and tore apart what was left of their robes to make crude loincloths. A part of Jehoshaphat felt like weeping from the pain of the humiliation of being exposed to the contempt of a whole nation. He did not give in to the urge, and he could see that Eleazar was burning with anger and hatred.

All kinds of filth had been thrown over them on the way out of the city: they looked worse than the most unkempt beggar. But what most preoccupied Jehoshaphat was what had happened to Caleb.

"Could they have killed Caleb?"

It seemed that Eleazar had been thinking on the same subject.

"If they'd killed us, then they would have killed him too, I suppose. But I don't think they'd kill just him. It's more likely that they'll keep him to sell as a slave."

That sounded right, thought Jehoshaphat. He continued in silence. Eleazar was curious, however.

"How did you come to have a Hebrew bondsman?"

"I bought him from a trader in Tyre. He'd been captured as a boy in a raid."

"You could have given him back to his kinsfolk straight away."

"I could have, Eleazar. But I meant him to work for his freedom. He would have had it at the end of the seven years, quite soon too."

As they came to the bend in they road turned for a last look at Rabbeh of the Ammonites. Eleazar lifted his right hand and cursed the city and its folk.

"When next I see you, Rabbeh, let this right hand tear down your stones: let this right hand lay your warriors in the dust and lead your women to captivity and throw your children from your walls: else let this right hand wither!"

Yes, thought Jehoshaphat, that's probably what will happen now. War and death and destruction. He clasped Eleazar's hand in comradeship. "Come on. This is going to be a long walk."

They turned the corner and left Rabbeh behind them. At that moment a small stone landed in the dust at Jehoshaphat's feet. His first thought was that some of the townsfolk had followed them to torment them further, or even stone them to death. But as he looked up to the slope above the road he saw to his delight a familiar face.

"Caleb!"

The servant was beaming as he made his way down towards them, and, wonderfully, he was leading their horses. Both men embraced him warmly.

"You're a sharp one, Caleb. How did you get away without a shave?"

"Servants talk to each other much more than their masters do, you know. The chamberlain's butler warned me that they were cooking up some sort of public show with you in it – they'd sent out to gather the crowd – so I had time to get the horses from the stables and slip away while the crowd was gathering."

"You didn't think of getting a message to us, by any chance?"

"Of course I tried, but your room was sealed off. The guards wouldn't let me pass, so I thought this was the best I could do for the cause of Israel."

They grinned in agreement.

"We'll have an easier trip to Jericho than if you'd hung about."

On the journey to Jericho Jehoshaphat had time to wonder whether Hanun's officials had connived at Caleb's escape with the horses. Granted that they had not wanted to kill them, it was in no-one's interest to have them making their way slowly across the country, and, perhaps, being killed on the way by zealous Ammonites. On balance he decided that there hadn't been much planning or foresight in the whole episode on Hanun's side, and Caleb's escape was fortuitous.

Caleb had managed to take a water flask with him at least, and some bread. Nonetheless, they had hard lying by the roadside that night.

The ground under his shoulders was uneven and the night had been colder than he had expected. By the time Jeho opened his eyes dawn was starting to break. Caleb was already seeing to the horses. They all felt sorry for themselves, he was sure, and he knew how dangerous that could be on a mission that still had danger potential.

"Eleazar - stop lazing about, Caleb's already at work!"

The big man grinned and looked round the whole circle of the horizon. Jeho wondered if he knew he was doing it.

There was nothing to eat that day, at least until they came to a Gadite farm, where they were received as honoured guests by the farmer. His dogs were more suspicious of the ragged half-shaven travellers. The goats, who had more reason to be suspicious than the dogs, showed no interest, but one of them was soon picked out by the farmer for the evening meal.

While they were eating, the farmer's children stared in fascination at the ambassadors. One little boy who had not yet reached his second birthday stretched out his hand to feel Eleazar's half-beard.

Jehoshaphat was not looking forward to writing this message: quite apart from the usual burdensomeness of reporting a failure there was the personal humiliation to bring up as well. The thing had to be done and it had to be done immediately.

"Lord king, when we had delivered your message the Ammonites seized us and shaved our beards and cut our garments so as to display our nakedness: they handled us roughly and cast us out of the city: all this was done on the orders of King Hanun."

That would do for now. He could rely on the messenger to pass on the details of their bizarre half-beards. The sight of a child giggling and running away round a door in his hoist's house persuaded him that the next order of business was a shave.

The more Jeho thought about what had happened, the less he understood it. It had been a normal diplomatic mission up to the point where things had turned sour. They were properly mandated diplomats, and in any case, if there had been any doubt about their mandate, the court officials could have addressed the point directly. The story about their being spies seemed ridiculous. All diplomats took back information to their kings: the point was that they had to get the information in a legitimate way. It was one thing for a diplomat to keep his eyes open; it was another thing to bribe officials for copies of secret papers. Jeho could think of nothing they had done that possibly be interpreted or misinterpreted as spying. The whole episode was completely inexplicable, except on the assumption that Hanun wanted to wreck relations with David. He discussed it with Eleazar in case there was something he had missed but both agreed that the charge of spying was unjustifiable. All they had seen that could be considered as sensitive was the royal armoury, and it had been the chamberlain's own idea to take them there.

A message soon arrived from David, telling them to stay at Jericho till their beards had grown before returning. The same messengers told Jehoshaphat to expect his wife soon. That night should be his last solitary one before Deborah's arrival. Once the idea of her arrival formed in his mind, he could hardly wait to hold her again.

But that evening dinner was still with Eleazar, while Caleb waited on them.

Eleazar said, "I have a confession to make, and it is directed to you, Caleb."

Both Jeho and Caleb were surprised.

"What can you have to confess to me, Eleazar?"

"When you followed Rebecca from her house that night – I was the one who put an end to your enquiries. Do forgive me."

"Of course Caleb forgives you, Eleazar." Caleb looked less certain than Jeho.

"But why would you hit him for following Rebecca?"

Jeho realized the answer as soon as the words were out of his mouth.

"So Rebecca and you – so she wasn't in Ahithopel's plot at all?"

"I don't know about any plot of Ahithopel's – although I can't say I'd be surprised at anything that shifty worm got up to. No – I think you can expect Rebecca to be leaving Marion's service very soon indeed. She will be entering my household as soon as I can arrange it."

"If she'd been promised to anyone else that would be unlawful, you know. Guilt offering of one ram."

"Well, she hasn't been promised to anyone else. But the situation is not fully resolved yet, so it seemed prudent to keep it dark."

Jeho was amazed at this revelation. But then – why not? She was certainly a beautiful woman, with verve and subtlety if no dowry. Eleazar must be marrying for love.

Deborah arrived at Jericho the following evening in a carriage drawn by four horses: on any other occasion Jehoshaphat would have found that extravagant. As things were, he would have paid a far higher price to hold Deborah in his arms that evening.

Jeho took a moment to enjoy the sight of his wife. She stepped down with the same poise and dignity as though she had been attending the king at Jerusalem. She was wearing a blue mantle embroidered with gold thread, with three gold bracelets on her left arm and two on her right. Her deep dark eyes pierced him with a mixture of affection and joy. There was something else to clear out of the way, he knew. She had been through fear, and he knew Deborah well enough to imagine the anger she would have conceived.

Anger that has no-one to be directed against can come out in strange and unexpected directions, he knew.

Deborah pulled back from his embrace and examined his face as if disappointed.

"So you tidied yourself up then?"

"I shaved all over my face if that's what you mean."

They held each other for longer, each thinking things could have been much worse.

After their dinner they soon retired to their private room on the pretext of Deborah's tiredness after her journey.

"I've never been to Jericho before. Why doesn't it have a city wall and gates?"

"Joshua cursed it after the Israelites conquered it. No-one dares rebuild the gates and wall. But the site is too good to leave alone, here at the fords of the Jordan above the Salt Sea."

"All that time ago? Moses' days? It's surprising even so that no-one has rebuilt the wall."

Something was preying on Deborah: Jehoshaphat saw how her fingers were twisted around the tassels of her head-dress and heard her dry throat.

"Will it come to war?"

"No doubt of it. They know what they've done and they can't back down now. I imagine Hanun would do differently if he were to face the same choice again, but now it's too late. His people would never fight for him again if he paid David tribute now."

"I mean – for us. Will you go to the war?"

"That depends on the king. If he goes, so do I."

She stared into Jehoshaphat's eyes.

"I've already lost enough to the king's service. I don't want to lose you as well. Your mother has made two husbands for me: can't I keep one of them at least?"

Jehoshaphat pulled her closer to himself on the couch. The memory of his elder brother never really left him either. He had done a brother's duty in marrying his deceased brother's widow, but often it felt as if Deborah and he almost had too much in common.

Humiliation and failure sometimes bring an unexpected peace in their wake. It was fitting that the time at Jericho turned into one of the happiest times Jehoshaphat had known. For two weeks he had no duties for the king except to grow a beard. He and Deborah enjoyed a long Sabbath free from the rounds of callers and influence-seekers and troubles that seemed major at the time and minor afterwards. They ate long cool evening meals, drank deep cups of wine, rode around the lakeshore of the Dead Sea and commiserated with the commander's attempts to bring his command up to battle readiness without disturbing the daily life of the city.

One afternoon Deborah was stretched out with her arms above her head on a couch.

"I really think sometimes we should spend more time on the farm, away from Jerusalem."

Jeho replied, "Perhaps so, but it wouldn't be as relaxing as this. We have responsibilities there. Everything the overseer decides for himself now he'd bring to us: there'd be disputes to settle, boundaries to confirm, servants to discipline..."

"I suppose you're right. I'd miss all the talk after a while too. But I'm enjoying this all the same."

One day he saw the farmer from the Gadite country who had entertained them: it was easier for Jeho to recognise him than for him to recognise Jeho. He had come to market to buy a ram, which Jeho insisted on buying as a gift for him.

After two weeks Deborah was content with his beard again, and so it was time to show it to the king.

On their last excursion to the Salt Sea – ostensibly to exercise the horses but really to enjoy each others' company with no-one else present – they found a spot to sit on the mats Caleb had packed for them and eat some figs. The conversation turned again to the time in Rabbeh: Jeho tried to communicate how horrifying the temple of Moloch had been. In some ways that had been a worse horror than the public abuse they had suffered.

"But surely you knew about the Ammonites sacrificing children? Everyone knows about that, don't they?"

"Yes, of course I knew - but it's different when you enter that dark poisonous temple of theirs and see the place where they burn them. I am never going to wipe that out of my mind."

Deborah was looking east over the Salt Sea and threw away a bad fig.

"Even so, is it so surprising? I mean, what do you expect? They aren't Hebrews and they don't have our law. Of course they do appalling things. They don't know any better."

"I don't think you can say that. The Almighty created us all. He didn't create us to have a law so that we can look down on others. They have to understand. When I think of that horrible temple and what goes on there - I just want to see it destroyed. Of course a lot of blood will be shed on both sides. But it's within our power to stop that evil at least."

She looked intently into his eyes.

"Is it really in your power? Of course our army can defeat theirs in battle, pull down their city walls and destroy their temples. You can grind their idols to dust, if the war goes that way. But can you take the worship of Moloch out of their hearts? Not even by killing them."

Jeho remembered the smooth official who had shown them the temple of Moloch, and the way he had bowed as he left the temple.

Eleazar was looking forward to the coming war. Usually it was enough for him that a foreign king was marching against David.

This time he had a personal hatred of the Ammonites, fuelled by humiliation.

On their last night in Jericho the commander entertained them.

"I heard someone say the other day that the Almighty fights for us. Is that what you think?"

Eleazar shook his head.

"I know that I can fight well and lead others to fight better than they otherwise would. But I do not think that the strength of my arm is what brings success, at least in some battles. I have known battles we have won that we should have lost, and I think that the Almighty was with us then. "

Deborah leaned over and looked Eleazar in the eyes.

"What makes the difference, Eleazar, is that you fight hard but without arrogance. He is with you because you are with Him."

"I think I know what you mean. I never like it when I hear people talk as if the Almighty owed us something, as if he were under obligation to us. It's as if my dog thought I was his servant because I feed him."

Deborah laughed and poured Eleazar more wine.

The commander and Jeho had been talking about how to gain information about the Ammonites from travellers when Eleazar burst out. "You talk as though battles were decided by knowledge. Sometimes they are. But more usually they're decided by something else."

"Which is?"

"The first man on either side who throws down his shield and turns and runs."

They all laughed.

"I mean it," insisted Eleazar. "You can know all you want to know about the enemy's strengths, how the land lies, what kind of chariots they have – but knowing all that never killed a fly. When a Philistine warrior runs at you with a spear it isn't what you know that counts. What counts is whether you can kill him before he kills you."

"Does knowledge count for nothing then, in your opinion?"

Eleazar frowned slightly.

"I didn't say that. It's often good to know the ground, so you can say that the enemy will have to come from either the north or the south, say. Although a good general will try to work out if he can come at you from the east, over the uncrossable mountains or unfordable river. But I say it again, you can know all you want. If they have four hundred to your hundred it doesn't matter that that you always knew what route they would take. What matters is that you can kill them three to your one and still lose."

Jeho noticed that Deborah was looking intently at Eleazar.

"I know what I'm good at, Deborah, killing people. At the right time."

"What is the right time for killing people?"

"Before they kill me."

Deborah nodded gravely: "Of course I'm glad about that. But what happens then?"

"What happens then? If they're lucky they get buried, otherwise something eats them. I go on to the next."

"That's what happens to the man you killed: I understand that. My question is what happens to his parents, wife, brothers, sisters, children? How many boys grow up knowing that a Hebrew warrior killed their father?"

"A lot, I suppose. That's war."

"And they grow up hating us for it. What kind of world does that make for?"

"The one we live in, where we are all at risk from sudden death."

Deborah looked grim: it was the end of the evening.

Jeho felt glad to see Jerusalem again, but apprehensive about the king. He was very conscious of having failed in his mission. He and Eleazar had been sent to improve relations with the

Ammonites. As he made their report David's face grew darker and he shifted in his chair, but his anger was not directed against them.

David recognized Eleazar and Jehoshaphat publicly, by giving them rings and making a proclamation in their honour.

It should have been the proudest of moments, when the trumpeter announced them on the palace steps and the king's words were read aloud.

"So much as the Ammonites dishonoured my servants, twice as much honour give I to them. So shall it be done to the men the king delights to honour."

The king himself embraced them as he gave them their rings.

Jeho was all too forcibly reminded of the scenes in Rabbeh to enjoy the moment.

ב

BETH

The second letter of the Hebrew alphabet

How can a young man keep his way pure? By living according to your word.

The atmosphere in the throne-room was sombre. There was no real discussion about what to do. It was clear that the decisions had already been taken. Joab reported that there had been a general levy of troops in the Ammonite lands. There were conflicting reports about the number of troops that Hanun had hired from his allies, but it was in the tens of thousands, and included charioteers. David commissioned Joab to take the army to Rabbeh, capture the city and depose king Hanun, fighting whatever troops and allies the Ammonites might have ready to defend themselves.

Since David was remaining in Jerusalem, Jeho and the rest of the courtiers would be at home too. At least that would be one piece of good news for Deborah, Jeho thought. And for himself? Did he want to be at home while Eleazar and the rest were having arrows and spears launched at them? He dismissed the uncomfortable question and concentrated on what was before him. David stood to give his blessing to Joab, who went onto one knee. He stood and the two men embraced. There was a general acclamation as Joab left the throne-room for his journey east.

Charioteers, thought Jeho. Just what we aren't so good at - fighting on plains against chariots. If we could fight on our terms it would be in hill country, on foot. What we are good at is the kind of fighting that requires discipline and individual initiative, not big set-piece manoeuvres with chariots. Not for the first time, he remembered Jonathan climbing up a cliff with his armour-bearer and wiping out a company of Philistines. He thought what a gap Jonathan had left.

The audience broke up and the king retired to his chamber. Jeho and the rest of the courtiers made their way out of the throne-room. He overheard a conversation between two other officials.

"Can we fight all of them at once? Not just the Ammonites but their allies as well?"

It was the secretary who was speaking.

"I'm not so worried about the Arameans. Their men are fighting because their king took a thousand talents of silver from Hanun. They aren't fighting to protect their homes and families and crops, which is what the Ammonites will be doing."

"If it comes to that, why are our troops fighting? The Ammonites mistreated two ambassadors: unlawful of course, but how many people need to die for that?"

Jeho thought that someone must have forgotten he was there, but he sympathised with the point. He wouldn't have wanted anyone to die for his sake either, but there was no need to interrupt.

"If it was only about two ambassadors we wouldn't be here. The point is that David can't tolerate a hostile country to his east. If they were prepared to be friendly we could live in peace with them. Not if they want to close off all contacts."

The secretary caught sight of Jeho, blushed, muttered an apology and bowed to allow him through the door.

Jeho thought about the army commander who would take the central part in the campaign. There was a shadow over Joab, and it was the mark of Cain. In the confused period when David was consolidating his throne, Joab had murdered Abner to avenge his brother Asahel. Joab had not been punished for this crime, but the guilt of it would never leave him.

Eleazar was making the rounds of the guard positions: not as a duty but to keep them cheerful and alert. Someone caught him by the elbow.

"May I speak with you, Eleazar?"

The speaker was a court official in his mid-forties, with grey patches of hair behind his ears and a half-grey beard: Eleazar remembered he was called Joel.

"Certainly." They moved into a corner of the courtyard, and Joel looked up earnestly at Eleazar:

"It's about my son, Jeremiah."

"Do I know him?"

"No, but I hope you will get to know him. He wants to join the army for the war on the Ammonites, and I want him to go to war with you."

"There isn't much I can do for him. Do you think he'll be safer with me than with anyone else?"

"Yes, I do think that. There are few other soldiers that can be named in the same breath as you."

"Perhaps. But in the heat of battle he'll still have to take his own chances. I'll meet the lad though."

Joel beckoned over his son, who had been waiting some distance behind him. Jeremiah was a bright-eyed young man with a wispy beard.

Eleazar nodded to Joel and drew away Jeremiah for a private conversation.

"You have to understand that I can't keep you alive in battle. I'll have my own fight to manage. All I can promise is that if some Ammonite does kill you, I'll do my best to kill him before he can strip your armour."

Jeremiah looked as if he wasn't sure whether Eleazar was joking but he clearly decided to take the older man seriously.

"What do you need to know? Never get isolated. Especially, never get isolated following a retreating enemy: the feigned retreat is the oldest ruse in war but it still works. Obey orders. Your captain's right even when he's wrong. A company of men doing the same thing hurts the enemy far more than fifty men doing the right thing. If we're in a night action make sure nothing can clink or rattle, including your tongue. Remember that most battles are lost because one army gives up just before the other one. Don't be the first to break. Show me your sword."

Jeremiah slid the sword out of its scabbard.

"Next time I ask you for your sword you can give it to me hilt first."

Eleazar touched the edge to his left arm.

"I wouldn't use this to shave a pig."

The young man's face soured.

"It'll have to be sharper than this when you meet your first Ammonite. You want to cut his throat, not club him to death. But point beats blade. Can you remember all that?"

Jeremiah returned his smile with a rueful grin.

"I seem to remember that you got yourself isolated on one occasion - and you couldn't get your sword out of your hand afterwards."

"It's true. But I was already one of the Three by then. You have a long way to go before you're ready to face a Philistine war-band on your own."

The only help Eleazar had had that day had been in stripping the dead of their valuables.

Eleazar was not in general an introspective man. The sight of a jagged white scar on his thigh took him back to the battle where he had taken the wound, and given a worse one back. He recalled the noise of battle, the sudden movement on all sides of spears, arrows, swords, shields all calling for attention, the shrieks of the wounded and the shock when a sword stroke cut open his leg, before the straight sword thrust he had given the Philistine between his teeth. He had survived many such fights, but one day, probably, it would be his turn to cough out his life's blood into the dust.

Now he had Rebecca to care for, and Rebecca who cared for him.

Few good things could happen in war for women. For men there was at least the chance of plunder, the chance to win distinction, the chance of higher command. For women there was the possibility of being bereft or widowed, and at worst the possibility that enemy soldiers would pour through the city gates or over its walls, with spears in their hands and spite in their hearts, to kill, rob, rape and enslave the losing side. The best a woman could hope for in war was that all those close to her survived and that life continued more or less as before.

It was becoming clear to Eleazar that he had always lived for the esteem of his fellow soldiers, and most of all for the esteem of the king. But a whole world was opening up for him beyond the world of horses and stores and weapons; now he had a hearth and in time he hoped to hold his child in his arms. He had never had any reason to throw his life away, but now he had many more reasons to preserve it.

Abishai was one of the very few men from whom Eleazar would take orders. He was Joab's brother, but that was not why he was recognised as a leader. He had authority because he had won their respect. He had beaten the Edomites at the battle of the Valley of Salt. Even more important perhaps, he had been David's companion in the old days when he was hunted down by Saul. On one occasion, they had made their way into Saul's heavily guarded camp and stolen a water jug from beside his head. David had restrained him that night: no-one was going to restrain him now. Abishai was ready for the fight, as they all were.

Eleazar found himself sitting next to Benaiah at the morning briefing. He was explaining to the captain on his other side how the Ammonite strategy was wrong.

"Our strategy would have been different. If an army is on the move, it's vulnerable to being harried in all sorts of ways. You can strike at the transport - small bands to go in and lame horses at night, burn carts and that sort of thing. You can ambush them in narrow places, hit them at the rear of the column to distract them, pretend to retreat to pull their lines out - but we've had none of that."

"Are they hoping we'll go to sleep? And then they'll start harassing the movements?"

"It's possible. But I think they've left it too late."

Joab called his captains to order. The strategy of the Ammonites and their allies was to catch the Hebrews between hammer and anvil: the anvil being the Ammonites themselves directly beneath the city walls of Medeba and the hammer being the Aramean forces on the plain.

Joab's plan was to blunt the impact of the Aramean charioteers by using his heavy infantry: the pikemen from Judah and Naphtali. Instead of standing their ground in an unbroken wall some of them would fall back to prepared positions, leaving a gap for the Aramean charioteers to race into. They would take it as a retreat by the Hebrews, which they could exploit. Once there were enough chariots in the trap, the pikemen would close off the gap, with Benjaminite archers to help hold it secure, and pick off the charioteers, who would be brought to a standstill by the heavy infantry.

The plan called for iron discipline on the part of the part of the infantry, who would have to execute the difficult manoeuvre of a controlled partial withdrawal. If they started to run from the chariots there would be a contagious panic in the Hebrew ranks.

"The Aramean force is out towards Medeba."

"Abishai - you take command of the main force and engage the Ammonites in front of the walls."

"What will you do?"

"I shall take on the Arameans. I think ten thousand Hebrews will be enough to beat them, if they're all experienced men. But if you see that we're losing, come to reinforce us. Similarly, I shall come to reinforce you if needed. Be strong and let us fight bravely for our people and the cities of our God. He will do what is good in his sight."

There was a murmur of agreement: the brothers embraced. Joab's adjutant quickly gave orders to select the hundred experienced companies that Joab had asked for and to get them into position against the Aramean army.

Joab had used some of the Thirty for commanding companies that would have to fall back to lure in the enemy. Eleazar agreed with Abishai that he also would take command of one of those infantry companies.

Slightly to his surprise Asahel, the sturdy thickset man he was supplanting as captain of the company, welcomed him warmly.

"Good to have you with us, Eleazar."

They quickly set up their fall back positions by heaping rocks into low ridges. Although a man on foot would be able to climb them without difficulty, they were an obstacle to chariots. They would therefore tend to force the chariots to go deeper into the funnel that would open up for them. Also, a man standing on top of a ridge would be at nearly the same height as a charioteer.

Once the positions were prepared they returned Eleazar brought his men back to the front rank. In the meantime the other companies who were not to form part of the fallback operation had been under orders to distract the enemy's attention from the preparation of the fallback positions, by making a lot of noise and dust without very much real activity.

Here they were, ready for action. Eleazar checked his own equipment: sword, shield, spear: all was in order. He checked the men closest to him, and told them to check the others in turn. The captains of ten reported that all men were ready. Now there was nothing to do but wait.

Eleazar could see that they would not have to wait long. The clouds of dust in the middle distance told him that the chariots were already on their way.

The final moments passed quickly. Absurdly, the image of a girl floated into Eleazar's mind, with a memory of a golden autumn evening in a walled garden years and years back: he shook himself back to concentration, determined not to miss the horn signal that would tell them when to fall back. Not too soon, he thought. We have to let them engage us and make it seem as if we are falling back as a result of their attack and not because we want to draw them in. He knew it would be difficult to think about anything else once the fighting started.

As the chariots approached, he thought he heard Joab growling his order to the archers.

"Hold it, hold it - now!"

The arrows whizzed out into the chariots, doing damage without any doubt, but still they came on. Now they were up with the front ranks: Eleazar leapt aside to avoid plunging hooves, and thrust his spear into the face of the chariot driver. Without a driver, the horses were panicking: Eleazar saw one of his men cut down the chariot's other occupant who was scrabbling after the reins. He shouted, "Keep your ranks!"

More chariots were joining the fight now, and the confusion was growing. He was relieved to hear the horn.

"Fall back, there, come on, fall back on me!"

They fell back on either side as men recalled their instructions, and the charioteers started to exploit the opening that they saw in front of them. The Hebrews fell back to their ridges: some turning and running, but most facing the enemy as they retreated, keeping up a field of spear points in the faces of the charioteers.

"Where is that ridge?" Eleazar wondered but then he saw the lines clear up. The plan had worked more or less as intended and about five hundred chariots were inside the funnel: now Joab had ordered heavy infantry across the mouth, with archers deterring the charioteers outside from reinforcing their comrades. The battle started to turn into a massacre of the surrounded charioteers, who soon found that their chariots were useless inside the long narrow killing funnel Joab had drawn them into. Spears picked off man after man until the last few charioteers were fighting on foot in the centre of a general mêlée.

Broken planks, pieces of shattered wheels, horses plunging about struggling to free themselves from the wreckage of chariots, wounded and dying charioteers - all added together to make a picture of confusion. Eleazar knew all about the confusion of war from long experience: he knew that nothing ever works out quite as expected. This plan was working out better than most. The Aramean charioteer in from of him had dismounted from his chariot, an overturned wreck, and was mounting a determined defence with his back to it. He turned aside Eleazar's initial spear-thrust with his sword, and Eleazar had to whip his head back to avoid the back-stroke. He body-checked the Aramean while he was still completing the move: the man stumbled onto his left knee. The Aramean rolled forward into Eleazar's legs to knock him over: Eleazar leapt over him and ran his spear into the man's neck. The spear snapped off in the Aramean's neck so that Eleazar had to use the man's own sword to finish him off.

When he looked up it was more or less over. He climbed onto the wrecked chariot for a for a better view, and could see the uncommitted Aramean reserves making off as fast as they could, kicking up clouds of dust from their chariots. The foot soldiers had not got so far but were heading the same direction.

He jumped off the chariot and nearly stumbled over a body on the sand. It was Asahel lying there, but he had no head.

I always hate this part, Eleazar thought. Someone has to see to it, though. Each unit had to bury its own Hebrew dead, and the Aramean bodies would be released for burial if anyone came to request them under truce conditions. There was no sign of that, so the senior Hebrew officers would have to make arrangements.

One of the bodies was an Aramean captain with a dagger in the back of his neck. Eleazar suspected that he had been killed by his own men; probably because they thought he would try to stop them from deserting. Or perhaps someone had used the confusion of battle to pay him back for some old insult. The truth of it would most probably never come out, he thought.

Eleazar was glad that Jeremiah had come through the battle without a scratch.

ר

RESH

The twentieth letter of the Hebrew alphabet

Many are the foes who persecute me, but I have not turned from your statutes.

Jeho thought that the atmosphere was always a little strange at court when there was a foreign war and the king was at Jerusalem. It felt as though the real action was elsewhere: maps were sought after and messengers from the front were eagerly questioned. The court's attention turned outwards for a change.

"General Joab has returned in person, lord king. I understand that the success has been so complete that he has returned for further instructions."

Joab was ushered straight into David's inner chamber. He had a major success to report.

"We have beaten the Arameans, lord king. They have been scattered off the plain and retreated beyond the river."

"What about the Ammonites?"

"They have retreated inside the city. They are doing nothing other than defending the walls of Rabbeh."

There was a sound of commotion outside; someone was shouting, desperate to be admitted.

Jeho went out and saw two footmen arguing with a dusty and dishevelled messenger. He thought the man should be admitted. He ushered him in and the messenger spluttered out, "The Arameans are going to fight again!"

Joab looked annoyed.

"Give your message properly, man."

The messenger recollected himself.

"My lord king, Shobach has regrouped the Aramean forces at Helam. They are getting ready to fight again."

Joab said, "I thought they had had enough."

David stroked his beard.

"Perhaps Hanun asked for his silver back. He might think they didn't do enough to earn it first time."

Joab made a noise that might have been agreement. David looked Joab in the eye.

"This time I shall go in person and take command in the field."

Joab embraced his king.

This time Jeho would be part of the army, at least as part of the king's personal staff. As usual, he would be responsible for a large part of the co-ordination of effort required to raise the levy of men of fighting age and move them and their supplies to the battlefield.

Jeho thought of going to the perfume shop on his way home, but he thought better of it. It was much better to give Deborah expensive presents when things were going well. She would not be grateful for a present, however expensive, that was meant to soften the blow of bad news.

As he passed by the perfume shop, Marion came out. She had a small but elaborately wrapped jar in her hands. He asked about the vineyard. Marion's face brightened.

"Lord Jehoshaphat, I think we are going to be able to keep the vineyard. Ahithopel sent a messenger yesterday. He told us that his master was no longer interested in buying the vineyard, and he was withdrawing his offer. We were trying to work out why he has changed his mind."

"So there is no risk of any accusation against you or Shimron?"

"No, all that seems to be behind us now. We can just look forward to the wedding of Zilpah and Shimron."

When he got home that evening, there was no need to tell Deborah the news. As soon as she saw his face she said, "You're going to the war, aren't you? Everyone says the king is going to Rabbeh."

There was a look of pain on her face that Jehoshaphat had rarely seen. It saddened him to think that he had to confirm her worst fears.

"You know that's what I told you. If the king goes to Rabbeh, then I go with him."

She screamed back at him.

"I know that's what you told me! Do you think that makes it any easier?"

Now she was in tears, her shoulders heaving. Jeho embraced her and they stood in each others' arms for a long time without speaking.

That evening they felt closer to each other than they had done since the days of leisure at Jericho. There were many things he could say: that his duties were mostly administrative, and there was every reason to think that the war would go well for the Hebrews, but there was no way to disguise the fact that he was going to war and death was a real possibility. There were tears in Deborah's eyes when she saw him off the next morning, and Jeho felt like weeping too. As he made his way to the palace, he forced himself to think about the campaign to come.

The commander of the levy would be Asama. His relationship with Joab was a difficult one, which made the presence of David desirable if not essential.

The whole world seemed to be going to war. Wherever he looked there were arms and armour, carts and barrels, donkeys and horses, all being led, pushed or ridden by all sorts and conditions of men. A one-legged man swung himself up into a cart stacked with baskets of grain, a boy perched perilously on top. A powerful scent told him that another cart that was just going past was stacked with onions, some of which had been crushed in loading.

When he heard the king was coming, Eleazar wondered how Joab would react to David's taking over command in person. Some commanders, he was sure, would react with a kind of exaggerated deference, referring the most routine questions to the king. Others would set up a more or less open power struggle for the loyalty of senior commanders. He did not expect Joab to go down either route. He was, Eleazar believed, loyal enough to David to accept his broad strategic plans while exercising active command under his authority. At least, that was the outcome Eleazar hoped for.

The decisive battle took place at Helam. The Hebrews knew that the Ammonites were on a defensive footing in Rabbeh. They could concentrate on the Arameans. The enemy still had more chariots than the Hebrews could muster, but Joab thought that their morale had been dented by defeat.

The important point about chariots was that their advantages of speed and mobility could be countered by forcing them onto difficult ground. There was no time for the Hebrews to prepare a defence, but David had identified a wadi they could use.

Eleazar mustered his company again.

"We've beaten the Arameans before. Now we have to do it again. They're fighting because their king took money from the Ammonites to fight. They will yield before we do. Fight now, for David and for Asahel!"

The fighting quickly became confused. A number of chariots fell over the edge of the wadi. Two chariots collided: their wheels and teams became entangled in a pile of confusion. Horses whinnied and kicked. At least one of the chariot drivers was dead: it was possible that the accident happened because he had been killed by an arrow.

A group of chariots - not an organised squadron, it seemed, but just those who happened to be nearest - drew up around the fallen chariots. Several men dismounted to see to the wreckage. They formed a defensive circle around the man who emerged from the wreckage. It was their general, Shopach.

Hebrews raised their spears ready for the word to cast. Arrows were swiftly notched. The remnant of the Aramean force would probably die without anyone having to come near them.

Eleazar did not want to see brave men die needlessly. Their general was the only man who could stop the killing. He shouted across to Shopach.

"Shopach! Your men are dead by the thousand. Your allies are no help to you. Give yourself up to the mercy of King David!"

"Never! If your king wishes me to be his prisoner, he can defeat me in single combat first."

The troops fell back. David himself responded to the challenge.

"So be it."

David was a more formidable figure than when he had first gone to war, against Goliath of Gath, so many years ago. The battle-hardened king was armed with more than a sling: he carried a bronze sword and wore functional and deeply-scored armour. Shopach approached warily, balancing lightly on the balls of his feet.

A wild scything stroke came from Shopach. David ducked beneath it and in that moment stabbed upwards.

David's sword plunged into Shopach's stomach. Shopach's arms grabbed reflexively towards the wound and his sword caught David over the helmet, but it wasn't a real stroke. The sword fell from Shopach's hand as David drew his sword out of the wound.

Shopach fell onto his knees. Blood welled out of his mouth. The sand beneath him was dark with blood. David moved to his right, leaving room for the stroke that would remove Shopach's head.

David grabbed Shopach's hair in his left hand: the sword in his right swept down and severed the hairy neck. He held up the bleeding head to shouts and cheers from the Hebrews. Blood ran down his left arm.

Eleazar thought about the wildness of Shopach's last stroke and wondered if Shopach had wanted to survive his last duel.

Perhaps dying at the hand of David was preferable to returning to Hadazezer, to tell him that his army had been lost for a thousand talents of silver.

The remaining Arameans surrendered without further fighting: the duel had settled the issue, as perhaps Shopach had intended.

The army could return to Rabbeh.

They came to the place in the road where Caleb had surprised them when they were fleeing half-naked from their humiliation at the hands of the Ammonites. Around the next bend they would see Rabbeh. Eleazar drew himself up to his full height: his attentiveness communicated itself to his horse, who pricked up his ears. The hated walls of Rabbeh, which he had last seen from this very bend in the road, reminded him of the curse he had flung out against the city and its folk. Blood had already flowed at Medeba and at Helam. The war still had more of its course to run.

The king called Jeho over to him.

"Jeho, I want you to receive the surrender of king Hadazezer and his under-kings. You can have Eleazar and twenty of my guard as an escort. Hadazezer can keep his crown, but he must swear fealty to us, and pay tribute."

David handed Jeho his ring as a token of his commission: Jeho, even while his lips thanked the king for the honour of the embassy, as usual began his mental checklist. Inform Eleazar, draw up surrender terms, prepare to withdraw quickly if they refuse the terms, horses, provisions for an overnight stay, nominate a herald who knows the way, and so on.

"Do you think Hadazezer will surrender?"

"If he doesn't he'd better keep an eye on his own courtiers."

Eleazar nodded in agreement.

"The Ammonites are on their own now. The noose is tightening around their necks."

"Israel is as good as undefended right now. The garrison of Jerusalem is a few score men, with the help of the oldsters. We must get a significant number back home as soon as possible."

There was an enemy left to defeat, safe for the moment behind the hated walls of Rabbeh. But it was an enemy without allies and opposed by a battle-hardened army accustomed to winning. David could well afford to leave Joab in command of the forces in the field, with a sufficient force to keep the Ammonites shut up for the winter. As so often, the war revolved around agriculture. Enough of David's men could get back home for the harvest to be gathered in: the Ammonites were forced to leave their fields, or such as hadn't been destroyed, for their enemies. One way or another, that would affect the size of the force the Hebrews would have to face the following spring.

Jeho and Eleazar were used to mistrustful looks in a foreign town and were not likely to be upset by mere grimaces. Hadezezar received them courteously enough and summoned his chamberlain and priest to witness the terms of the surrender. He swore fealty to David and they arranged for payment of the tribute at the next new moon. They were not invited to dinner, but Hadezezar sent them some figs and wine. Jeho thought that was just enough to count as symbolic hospitality.

Eleazar had a packet of dried meat and some bread, so they were comfortable enough. As they shared the wine he asked about Jeho's family.

"What I don't understand, Jeho, is what relation your family had to Deborah before she and your brother were married."

Marriage was rarely allowed to take property far outside the extended family grouping.

"They were not really related at all. Both her parents had died, and she inherited a lot of land. She was in a position to make a choice."

"So she was not a young girl, then?"

"No, she was about twenty when she met my brother."

"So how did he meet her?"

"It was through a trial when she inherited. She had a distant relative who claimed that he should have inherited instead. There wasn't any real substance to his case but it came to trial. I handled the case."

"So Deborah met your brother through you?"

"Yes, and after his death I married her in accordance with the law."

Eleazar reflected what a pity it was that was there was no one to inherit such a fortune. He moved on to another subject: "I remember when he died."

Some of the light that had been in Jeho's face when he was talking about Deborah disappeared from it.

"Were you at the battle?"

"Yes. He got cut off from the main force. There was a small group of them surrounded by Philistines. They gave a good account of themselves – killed four to one – but the Philistines got them in the end. We couldn't get near to relieve them."

"I know you would have saved him if you could."

Jeho thought about on the fighting to come, and whether Deborah would have to mourn another son of Ahilud. He wanted to continue his life with Deborah, to father children, to write his chronicle and to serve his king and country. He reflected that he and Eleazar had already passed through many dangers and were alive to tell the tale. He could not decide whether that made it more or less likely that they would continue to survive.

א

ALEPH

The first letter of the Hebrew alphabet

Blessed are they whose ways are blameless, who walk according to the law of the LORD.

Uriah's face was more worn than Jeho remembered it. His eyes were those of a man who has seen too many wounds and too much death. He had the discipline of a good soldier, looking after his horse first and then seeing to his own appearance.

Jeho offered him a clean tunic before his audience with the king but Uriah refused it and went in as he was. After Uriah had made his report about the army and the progress of the war David dismissed him telling him to go to his house and watch his feet. After he had left, David ordered a gift to be sent to him; a platter of delicate meats and a jar of sweet wine. Jeho heard later that although the gift that indeed been received by Bathsheba's servant, Uriah had not gone home. He had spent the night sleeping at the palace gate amongst the king's servants. He had rolled out his sleeping mat from his army kit and covered himself with his cloak as if he had been camped outside Rabbeh.

The next morning David asked after the soldier.

"Send a messenger to Uriah's household. I wish to see him again before he returns to Rabbeh."

"In fact he's still at the palace, Lord King. He did not go home last night."

"He didn't go home? Are you sure?"

The king seemed shocked.

"Bring him to me straight away."

It did not take long for Uriah to arrive. After welcoming him to the king asked, "Haven't you only just come here from Rabbeh? Why didn't you go home to your wife?"

The soldier drew himself tall and replied.

"The Ark and the Hebrews are staying in tents and my general Joab and all the army are camping in the open fields. How could I go to my home and my wife? As surely as you live I will not do such a thing!"

The king said, "I want you to stay one more day, then tomorrow I will send you back."

There was a dinner that evening with much food and even more wine. Again, Uriah slept on a mat among the servants in the palace and stayed away from his home.

The next morning, David took the unusual step of giving Uriah a private audience. He had asked Jeho to bring his writing materials in, but then he dismissed him. When Uriah came out from the king's presence, he wasted no time in getting his horse and riding off, with another man in company. Jeho could see that Uriah was carrying a letter, presumably a secret order from the king to Joab, but it was very unusual for the king to write it himself. Jeho, who had been on many diplomatic missions for the king, couldn't help wondering what the secret was that he could not be trusted to keep.

Deborah had little interest in the secret message entrusted to Uriah.

"It's Bathsheba I feel sorry for," she snorted, " she doesn't get to see her husband in spite of his spending two nights in Jerusalem. The king, of course, gets to see him three times. It shows where soldiers' priorities lie."

From Jeho's point of view, it was Uriah who had been presented to the king, rather than the other way around, but he thought better of pointing that out to Deborah. He chose a different approach.

"At least Bathsheba knows that Uriah is safe. If he had stayed out in the field and another messenger had come, she might not know that she was even alive."

Joab's favoured way to send messages was by a single horseman, lightly armed, riding fast, changing horses at each army camp. His messenger came to Jerusalem and was admitted for an audience. He told David all that Joab had sent him to tell.

"The men of Rabbeh made an attack on us out in the field, and then we counterattacked and got as far as the entry of the city gate. But we were exposed to the fire of the archers on the wall; and some of the king's troops were killed, among them your officer Uriah the Hittite."

David said to the messenger, "Tell Joab not to be discouraged, for the sword consumes one as well as another: besiege the city even closer, and conquer it."

Jehoshaphat reflected as he took down the words. He thought how the king had changed since he poured out the water from the well of Bethlehem.

"How used one grows to death, and to ordering men to war. I was nearly ordered to my own death, if the Ammonites had gone a little further. They might have decided to send us back in pieces instead of naked."

The king told the messenger to make all speed back to the army, stood and dismissed all present, indicating that he wished to be alone. Jehoshaphat thought that that was unusual too, but perhaps he had been harsh in judging David to be lacking in compassion for the men lost. He quickly caught up with the messenger and asked after Eleazar.

"He is safe and well, my lord Jehoshapahat, and he is the talk of the army for what he did that night after Uriah was killed. He recovered the body from under the city walls for burial."

"How was that possible?"

"He arranged for a mock attack with fire arrows on the opposite side of the city, to create a diversion. That gave him the time to recover Uriah's body. They say that Joab didn't know whether to commend him or discipline him at first, but when he saw how the men reacted there was no question."

The Ammonites might well have feared a night attack: they were something of a speciality of the Hebrews. They required disciplined and level-headed troops: unwilling conscripts were best deployed by daylight.

On his way home, Jeho thought how the beggars on the streets of Jerusalem reflected the state of the nation. When times were relatively normal – without too much fighting – there were the blind and those born lame. When the country was embroiled in a pitched conflict there were the war wounded instead. He wondered what happened to the blind and the lame then. They just seemed to slip out of view.

When the mourning was past, David made Bathsheba his wife. There were some notable absentees from the wedding festivities, which lasted the full seven days dictated by custom. Joab, of course, was in the field with the army. Eliam, her father, was absent for the same reason. Ahithopel, her grandfather, was there, however, and so was her brother Machir.

At the wedding festivities Jehoshaphat was formally presented to Bathsheba. He was aware of her connection with Ahithopel and was wary of her. She looked to have been under strain but being widowed more than accounted for that. He could see that she was not someone to have as an enemy: she gave the impression of being someone who understood a few things, but very well.

Jehoshaphat saw at the wedding festivities that there was a new servant in the palace waiting on the king. He asked about him. He was told that he was a new servant in the King's bedchamber, a replacement for the one killed at Rabbeh. His name was Ahilud, and he had been promoted from the kitchens on the recommendation of the butler.

Jeho later heard that Ahilud, the new servant in the king's bedchamber, had been promoted to his new job before the battle in which Uriah was killed. He had taken up his new duties immediately after Uriah had left Jerusalem on his journey back to Rabbeh after reporting to the king.

Jeho had a question on his mind and summoned one of the king's servants to help him with it.

"I am your servant to command, Lord Jehoshaphat."

"I wish to know you better, Ahilud. What were you doing before the king took you as a servant of the bedchamber?"

"I was working in the kitchen, my lord. Mostly it was cleaning fish, but I used to pluck birds and bone cuts of meat as well."

"How did the king know of you?"

"The butler recommended me, my lord. I believe he thought that I was a neat worker."

"It does both of you credit. What happened to your predecessor?"

"Nebo died in the war, my lord. He died at Rabbeh of the Ammonites, in the same battle as Uriah, the one everyone calls the Hittite."

"Did he know Uriah before, do you know?"

"I'm sure I don't know, my lord. I don't really think they could have had any contact."

"It is strange, isn't it? If he didn't volunteer, and if Uriah didn't ask for him, then the king must have sent him."

"I'm sure I couldn't say, my lord. Will there be anything else?"

"No, that will be all, Ahilud."

He bowed and left, closing the door behind him. Jeho reflected on a servant of the bedchamber sent into the heat of battle.

A lady of the bedchamber sent the message that the time was near for Bathsheba to give birth. Jeho arranged for a herald to be ready to make the announcement at the palace gates. Later on there would have to be heralds sent to the different parts of the country. Fortunately the king was already in Jerusalem. When one of the young maids entered with bowed head to tell Jeho that Bathsheba had given birth to a son, he had already prepared the proclamation. He sent the herald to make the announcement. He could not make an entry in the archives until the king had named the boy.

נ

NUN

The fourteenth letter of the Hebrew alphabet

Your word is a lamp to my feet and a light for my path.

"What were you reading when I came in?"

"About Moses. The bit where he made a serpent in the wilderness and lifted it up on a pole. I wanted to see if was as I remembered it."

"Was it?"

"More or less so. There was a plague and Moses made a brass serpent and erected it on a pole. Those who looked at it were healed."

"Why the interest?"

"I just think that there's something in the story that escapes me, that's all. I wonder if we're going to need something like that soon."

"Are you feeling ill, Deborah?"

"No. I didn't mean it like that." Deborah seemed to want to change the subject.

"I get the impression you don't much like the king's new wife."

Jeho wondered if Deborah wanted to play the game in which she pretended to be jealous.

"It's not for me to like or dislike her. But it's true enough – if you think of how Abigail is, for example, or how Michal used to be."

"I know what you mean." Deborah was frowning. "Michal used to be – well, queenly, really. You could see it in the way she came into the room, as if her presence was a gift she was bestowing on everyone there."

He laughed. "Yes, but it was, in a way. Bathsheba seems more – guarded. I suppose she has lost a husband recently, as well as gaining one."

"A lot of women have lost husbands. I wish we could stop having war after war. It's almost as if we have to have a new war every year, like the grape harvest but earlier."

"She is Ahithopel's granddaughter, I suppose. You'd expect something to rub off."

"Yes. Characteristics sometime skip a generation like that. She might be more like Ahithopel than his own children were. Of course you're thinking that she's a lot prettier than Ahithopel."

Jeho couldn't deny that he had been thinking exactly that, even if he hadn't been about to say so.

"She was a soldier's daughter as well as another soldier's wife. Her father is Eliam. So both her father and husband belonged to the king's mighty men."

"The king's mighty men. What an imposing collection of soldiers. I like Eleazar best, of course."

"Eleazar; he's the kind of man other men look up to – would like their sons to be, or in fact would rather like to be themselves."

"I'd rather have you than Eleazar. I'm not saying he isn't attractive, of course, in a rather obvious sort of way."

Jeho must have had a curious expression on his face, to judge from Deborah's giggle.

"But I couldn't have this sort of conversation with him. I don't know what sort you could have in fact, unless it was about his latest battles. "

"Eleazar isn't stupid by any means. Perhaps a bit – what would the right word be – tightly focused."

"What do you mean, tightly focused – concentrated on soldiering?"

"Not so much soldiering specifically, just everything that belongs to his service to the king. Benaiah's another one, but even more so. He's never off duty so far as I can see."

"There's something on your mind, isn't there?"

"I can't let go of the time Uriah came. When David sent the letter to Joab."

"Isn't it unusual for the king to write to Joab in his own hand?"

"Very unusual. Every other time he's sent a letter from Jerusalem to the field it was my job to write it."

"So what was different this time?"

Jehoshaphat shook his head slowly.

"So often there are things one doesn't know that make all the difference."

"How do you mean?"

"I'll give you an example. Eleazar told me, after the battle of the Valley of Rephaim about the fighting, how many Philistines they killed, how the king held them back for the ambush, all that sort of thing. What he didn't say - I found out from the king, after we came back from Rabbeh - was that the king waited to lanch the attack until he had a sign from the Lord, which was a kind of a noise in the mulberry trees, like a sound of walking feet."

"But I suppose only the king heard it?"

"Only the king interpreted it, at any event. Sometimes what's important isn't what you see or hear but what you understand from it."

"I think I know what you mean. To be older isn't necessarily to benefit from all one's experience."

"No. Do you know the armourer's shop - that one with all the bronze shields hanging in it?"

"Yes. I was in there with my friend Ruth the other day when she was buying a dagger."

Jeho frowned: "Is she planning to kill Zephaniah then?"

"Only if he deserves it. What happened in there?"

"There was once a moment in that shop when I caught a glimpse of something surprising among all the reflections around me. Then I realised two things at the same moment. One was that I had seen the reflection of my own face: the other was that I had taken it for that of my mother's brother."

"So you realised not only that you are getting older..."

"... but also that as I grow older I look more like the rest of my family. Exactly."

The next day, Jeho was on his way to the perfumer's looking for a present for Deborah. As he walked through the crowded streets, his thoughts were in a familiar groove. He had wondered time and again about the way in which Uriah had met his death. Why had Nebo been sent away to war? Only the king could have sent him. If the servant had offended the king in some way, that could account for it. There was no indication that that had happened. David had sent a favourite servant to a station of danger. Why would David do that? There was one obvious answer. The servant had learned something that must not come out. Perhaps Nebo had been meant to die. Jeho stopped dead in his tracks. If Nebo's death was not an accident, then perhaps Uriah's had also been intended. That was why he had written to Joab in his own hand. David had ordered Joab to make sure that the secret died with Uriah and Nebo. What was the secret? He remembered the proclamation, the birth of the child. It dawned on him that David had lain with Bathsheba while she was still Uriah's wife. That explained everything: why Uriah had to die, why Nebo had to die, why the king had written to Joab in secrecy.

Jehoshaphat felt as though someone had slapped him across the face. The shock drained all feeling from him; it was as if his guts had been pulled down into the ground. His thoughts kept revolving around the same circuit: David, Bathsheba, Uriah, Joab. Lust, adultery, deceit and murder. If only it could be not true. David, a king like any other king, to take what he wanted from his subjects. Samuel, he thought, I'm glad you did not live to witness what became of the shepherd boy you anointed to be king. Was David really no better than Hanun or Hadazezer?

He went home directly. Deborah knew that something important had brought him as soon as she saw his face, quite apart from the fact that he had come home in the middle of the morning. She dismissed the girl who was combing her hair: Jeho gave her the news in a low voice, sitting beside her with their heads almost touching.

"Who knows?"

"I don't know how many exactly. Joab, obviously. Probably a few very close to the king, like Benaiah."

"Bathsheba gets a baby nobody wants, while Michal would have given both her legs to have one. These things are so ... aleatory. Or perhaps not?" She was thinking aloud. "Could Bathsheba have intended it all along? Surely not."

"That would make Bathsheba someone quite different to what I imagined her to be."

"Quite. But that's not the same thing as 'can't possibly be true', is it?"

"She can't have *expected* that Uriah would ... die."

"Not so coolly, perhaps. But bearing a king's child - she knew David to be a man of action. Perhaps she thought he would make something happen, without being clear what. Something that would improve her position."

"It could have been something to prejudice her position. David might have had her killed instead of Uriah."

"She took a risk. It worked out for her. She might see her son on the throne one day. The king of Israel, Ahithopel's great-grandson."

"What are you going to do about this?"

"I have to tell somebody. I can't think who. Should it be the high priest?"

"I think you should see the prophet. Talk to Nathan."

"I have a duty to the king. David relies on me. I have always been loyal to David."

"For a long time, you haven't needed to decide whether your prime loyalty is to the king or to the Almighty. Now you must decide. If you are right, the king has broken God's law he has committed adultery and murder. The king is not above God's law. The prophet Nathan can call him to account for what he has done"

"I wish I could be sure."

"Why can you not say that to Nathan? Tell him that you aren't sure. Surely the Everlasting will tell him if what you say is true or not."

"I don't know. The Everlasting does not always do what we expect Him to do. The words of knowledge of the prophet do not come to order like a shopkeeper delivering fish."

"So what are you going to do?"

"I think you are right. Nathan should know."

It occurred to Jeho that he had talked about knowing. There was really no doubt in his mind any more.

The prophet Nathan lived in a small house close to the Tabernacle. Jeho went there without any appointment: he wanted to attract little attention as possible. The prophet himself answered the door. He did not seem surprised to see Jeho and ushered him in without a word. Jeho's mouth was dry under the unblinking gaze of the prophet.

"Nathan, I want to see you about a very difficult matter."

The prophet put his finger on his lips.

"I know you're a loyal man, Jehoshaphat son of Ahilud. What you have to tell me concerns the king, doesn't it?"

Jeho nodded.

"It does. It has to do with the war."

The prophet interrupted him.

"That is where the king should be. He should be leading his men in the field of battle."

Jehoshaphat said, "He stays here in Jerusalem and men are dying under the walls of Rabbeh. One who died recently was Uriah the Hittite."

"Soldiers do die in war, Jehoshaphat. It has always been so and always will be so."

"Certainly soldiers die in war. They die at the hand of the enemy. And sometimes their own commander exposes them to death at the hand of the enemy."

The prophet looked grave now.

"You mean that Joab intended Uriah to die?"

"It's worse than that. I think that the king ordered Joab to put Uriah in the forefront of the fighting to ensure his death."

"Why would the king wish that Uriah should die? He was a loyal soldier to the king."

"Uriah was indeed loyal, much more so than the king deserved. Bathsheba who was Uriah's wife has given birth to a child, but Uriah was not the father of her child."

There was a long silence. Then the prophet spoke.

"The Everlasting has taught me many things, by many different means. Sometimes His word comes to me through dreams or visions. At other times His word comes when I am meditating on the Scriptures. At other times His word comes through the mouth of a servant of the Lord. And that is what you are, Jehoshaphat. By speaking to me today you have served the purpose of the Everlasting."

ו

WAW

The sixth letter of the Hebrew alphabet

I will speak of your statutes before kings and will not be put to shame, for I delight in your commands because I love them.

It was hard for Jeho to meet David's eyes now. He had gone over his reasons many times, both in his own mind and with Deborah. It was inevitable that a man of his stamp would reflect long and hard and he was still convinced that he had done his duty in speaking to Nathan. His loyalty was to the king, but above the king to the Almighty and his law. His reason was satisfied but his heart was divided. It felt as though he had betrayed the king who had appointed and honoured him.

The day came when Nathan sought out Jeho at the palace to say that he was ready to confront the king, before the assembled court. Jeho took the message to David.

"Nathan requests an audience, lord king."

"Very good. Show him in."

"If you please, lord king, it might be more appropriate to receive him in the throne room. He wishes to bring a word of public importance, he says."

David breathed hard, but rose from his chair and went to the door in the opposite wall. Somehow the court had already assembled, and a salute went up as he entered. He acknowledged it and took the throne.

"Nathan, approach me and state your word."

The prophet's face was stern and his words even more so.

"King David, I have come to bear witness against one of our people."

A shiver of anticipation shook the room. This meant a trial. The witness was the person who brought charges against a person he believed to have offended against the law. David, tight-lipped, nodded to him to continue.

"There were two men who lived in the same town, one rich and the other poor. The rich man had great herds of cattle and flocks of sheep, but the poor man had nothing except one little ewe lamb that he had bought. He raised it and it grew up with him and his children. It shared his food, drank from his cup and even slept in his arms, so it was like a daughter to him. Now a traveller came to the rich man, but the rich man refrained from taking one of his own sheep or cattle to prepare a meal for the traveller who had come to him. Instead he took the ewe lamb that belonged to the poor man and prepared it for the one who had come to him."

David's spontaneous anger flared out.

"As surely as the Lord lives, the man who did this deserves to die! He must pay for that lamb four times over, because he did this and had no pity."

Nathan had bowed his head while this speech was continuing: his lips were moving. Slowly he raised his face and looked the king full in the eyes.

"You are the man."

"This is what the Lord, the God of Israel, says. "I anointed you king over Israel, and I delivered you from the hand of Saul. I gave Saul's house to you, and his wives into your arms. I gave you the house of Israel and Judah. And if all this were not enough, I would have given you even more. Why did you despise the word of the Almighty by doing what is evil in His eyes? You struck down Uriah the Hittite with the sword and took his wife to be your own. You killed him with the sword of the Ammonites. Now the sword will never depart from your house, because you despised me and took the wife of Uriah the Hittite to be your own. This is what the Almighty says: 'Out of your own household

I am going to bring calamity upon you. Before your very eyes I will take your wives and give them to one who is close to you, and he will lie with your wives in the open. You did it in secret, but I will do this thing in broad daylight before all Israel.'"

Jeho was holding his breath to see how the king would react. David's face was like stone. Then he stood from the throne and approached Nathan. Jeho wondered if he was going to strike him or even cut him down on the spot. Then David lowered his head in humility and said to Nathan, "I have sinned against the Almighty."

Nathan replied, "The Everlasting has taken away your sin. You will not die. But because by doing this you have shown utter contempt for the Lord, the son born to you will die."

Nathan left the palace. It was in a state of shock, like an ant's nest turned over by a shovel. Benaiah was ready to have Nathan arrested but the king confined him to the palace. A handmaiden was sent to check on Bathsheba and the child: rumours began to spread that both had been swallowed up by the earth, or struck by lightning. The word came back that the child had indeed fallen ill. Doctors arrived to attend the child.

The servant was obviously nervous.

"My lord Jehoshaphat," he said, "I am deeply concerned for the king. He has taken no food these three days."

"Go on. Has he slept?"

"He does not sleep in his bed, at least. He lies all night on the floor, but I do not think that he sleeps. He groans and cries out in ..."

The man stopped, obviously feeing that he was going too far.

"You can tell me. You were going to say that he cries out in the anguish of his mind?"

"I think that he is praying, Lord Jehoshaphat."

"Thank you. You are a true friend of the king in telling me this. I shall see what I can do."

Jehoshaphat carried in a platter of meat and fruits with his own hands after that. The king refused to eat at all. The elders of his household stood beside him to get him up from the ground.

On the seventh day the maid sitting by the child's cot became aware of a horrible stillness. The child had no breath to mist her bracelet. David's servants were afraid to tell him that the child was dead, fearing he might do something desperate.

David noticed that his servants were whispering among themselves and he realised the child was dead.

"Is the child dead?" he asked.

"Yes," they replied, "he is dead."

David got up from the ground. After he had washed, put on lotions and changed his clothes, he went into the tabernacle and worshipped. Then he went home, and ate a meal.

Jehoshaphat was concerned that the king might be mad.

"Why are you acting this way? While the child was ill, you fasted and wept, but now that he's dead, you get up and eat!"

David's face was set like a stone.

"While the boy was still alive, I fasted and wept. I thought the Almighty might be kind to me and let the child live. Now that he is dead, why should I fast? I will go to him, but he will not return to me."

There was one person in the palace who did not mourn the baby boy. Michal's unholy satisfaction at the death of the child was short-lived. David turned to his new wife Bathsheba in their joint grief and comforted her and she him.

ס

SAMEKH

The fifteenth letter of the Hebrew alphabet

Sustain me according to your promise, and I shall live; do not let my hopes be dashed.

Jeho was awakened by Caleb violently shaking his shoulder: "A summons to the palace; you're wanted on the King's business!"

"Quiet, you'll wake my wife. Any idea of the matter?" He bundled Caleb out of the bedroom to hear the reply: "A messenger arrived from Joab, the man says."

That explained the urgent nocturnal summons. A messenger from Joab would have instant access to the king at any hour of the day or night.

A sleepy Deborah appeared as they were about to leave for the palace.

"I suppose this is the king's business. Does David know what time it is?"

"I cannot say, dear wife, but I do know that he knows something new that he thinks I should know too."

"I just hope it's not another embassy. I still haven't recovered from seeing you clean shaven."

"I don't think you need worry about that. The time for diplomacy is long gone, at least as far as the Ammonites are concerned."

The streets were almost deserted at that time of night: most of the younger men were out in the field at Rabbeh and most citizens went to bed shortly after dark. Their footsteps rang loud on the pavements up to the palace. The guards had obviously been alerted to expect members of the king's private council: in spite of the late hour, they were directed to the throne room. Jeho had expected a meeting after midnight to be in the king's private chambers.

Jeho left Caleb outside the throne room. When he entered he saw that most of the king's counsellors were already there; Seraiah entered on his heels.

Jeho went to the box in the corner of the room where he kept a wax writing tablet for notes, which would be copied onto parchment later. The king looked at him approvingly; obviously he wanted a formal record made. Jeho noticed a small scroll lying on the king's lap.

"I have summoned you here at night and in haste because I have received a letter from the general. Joab writes: "I have fought against Rabbeh and taken its water supply. Now muster the rest of the troops and besiege the city and capture it. Otherwise I will take the city, and it will be named after me."

A broad grin lit the king's features.

"It seems to me that Joab's words point the way I have to take. Does any among you advise me to remain at Jerusalem?"

There was no vote for that course of action, as Jeho solemnly noted.

"It is my command that all this court, with all my remaining guards save a watch to defend against bandits, should decamp to Rabbeh at the third hour tomorrow. Make your arrangements, and prepare to bear arms beside your king!"

Not for the first time, Jeho reflected that the order was easier to give than to execute. It required horses, carts, provisions, arrangements for temporary command of the skeleton garrison of Jerusalem, a messenger to Joab...and it was what Deborah most dreaded. For all that, he was certain that the king had made the right choice.

It was as if the whole palace – even the whole city – gave a great sigh of relief to find itself the locus of purposeful and controlled activity with an aim in sight. There was loading of carts, horsemen riding off, writing of messages, valuables committed to safekeeping and lovers embracing for what might be the last time. Markets were scoured for oil and wine, barley and wheat. Armourers sold new helmets to soldiers going to Rabbeh and short daggers for their wives who would stay at home.

The sense of relief was not universal. Deborah could not hide her dismay.

"I hate the sound of the name of Rabbeh."

"Next week it might be called Joab if he carries out his threat."

The jest was not well received. Tears formed in Deborah's eyes as she turned her face away.

So David mustered the entire army and went to Rabbah. The king would lead the assault to capture the city.

Jeho arrived at the camp outside Rabbeh in the early evening with the king's reinforcements for the army. The next morning he asked Eleazar to show him Uriah's grave.

"It was a fine thing that you did, Eleazar, retrieving the body for burial."

"Uriah was a good soldier. I think he would have done the same for me."

"Yes, he deserved it. With what we know now, we can say that he deserved it even more than I knew."

The two men stood in silence for a moment, reflecting on the soldier, his wife and his king. Then Jeho picked up a stone and laid it on the grave as a mark of respect. They returned to the camp to prepare for the next day's battle.

After their final briefing in the king's tent Jeho and Eleazar joined the other men of Eleazar's company for their evening meal. Jeho had thought that he was not hungry, but the smell of the roasted lamb quickened his appetite. Jeho realised that there was a man around the campfire he had not seen before. He wondered if the man could be an Ammonite spy. He waited until there was a lull in the conversation. Then he called out to the man.

"You there, soldier! Have you ever met the king?"

The man in the shadows stirred uneasily.

"The king? The adulterer, you mean?"

A silence fell. "He has confessed his sin with Bathsheba," said Jehoshaphat. "The Everlasting does not hold it against him, and nor should you."

"I'm not talking about Bathsheba. The king took from me the only woman I ever loved. He took my wife."

"Your wife? How – or are you the one who...?"

"My name is Palti son of Laish," said the man with a quiet assertiveness. "Husband to Michal daughter of Saul."

"It was forbidden in the Law of Moses to take back a spurned wife. The king had no right to take her back."

For the first time during the conversation, Jehoshaphat caught sight of his face clearly in the firelight: it was the grim face of a man for whom life held little to hope for. He turned on his heels and passed out of the circle of light.

"Do you know what I'm afraid of, Jeho?" It came as a surprise to Jeho to hear Eleazar speaking of fear of anything he might face in battle.

"Tell me."

"I don't relish facing the ones you meet when hope has gone: the defenders who have lost everything they were fighting to protect. They tend to be fighting to die, not to kill."

Jeho wondered how he would feel if the situation were reversed: how it would be if Jerusalem were under siege with the Ammonites outside the walls, fighting their way through the gates, how if he had seen Deborah killed at the threshold of their house. Would he then be fighting to kill or to die?

Jeho allowed himself to contemplate his death. Before the next sunset Deborah might be a widow for the second time. At some point he would face an Ammonite, sword in hand, and one of them would spill the other's blood. He wished the Ammonite no ill, but he intended to be quicker than his opponent and return to Deborah.

Tomorrow's battle was not to determine the fate of Jerusalem, but of Rabbeh. How hard would the Ammonites fight for Hanun, their king of a few disastrous months? He remembered the jeering faces of the Ammonites on the day of his humiliation. Certainly they had little love for the Hebrews, but how many were prepared to die defending Hanun? They would know soon enough.

It was rumoured that Saul had seen a witch just before his last battle, and that he had been told of his impending death. Some ridiculed the story, pointing out that witches had been outlawed on pain of death. Jeho knew that the story was true, and he knew a lot more besides. He wondered if Hanun had soothsayers or diviners to consult, and whether they could tell what their master wanted to hear.

An hour before dawn runners were sent to each company to rouse the captains: half an hour before dawn the army was drawn up before the walls. All that Jeho could see was the company he was in (commanded by Eleazar) and those on either side. It seemed more natural to serve with Eleazar than directly in the king's bodyguard, which would have meant placing himself under the command of Benaiah.

Jeho recalled the final briefing meeting for the captains, the evening before. The king's tent had been uncomfortably crowded, the army being at full strength. Joab had set out the presumed situation of the defenders, whose provisions and water would be running low. The prisoners taken in the final stages of the siege had been interrogated and had revealed low morale and little personal loyalty to Hanun. Joab had done his best to lower the defenders' morale by making sure his men roasted lamb and beef within sight (if not within bowshot) of the ramparts. David had summed up by telling them to take nothing for granted and to prepare to face desperate and dangerous men. He himself would lead the final assault.

Jeho could now see the king wearing the same deeply-scored bronze armour he had worn to fight Shopach. He was speaking to Joab without looking at him, with his eyes on the ramparts. The plan was straightforward: a dawn assault with battering rams against the gate and siege ladders at other points around the walls to stretch the defence; archers covering the attack until the laddermen reached the ramparts. There was nothing in the plan that would surprise the Ammonites, but they would know that the battle could have only one outcome.

The city gates were of the old-fashioned kind, Joab had explained, set foursquare in the wall facing directly outwards. More elaborate constructions with dog-leg turns and double turns to hinder attackers were coming into use. The Ammonites had made an attempt to hinder access to the gates by building a wall, or rather barricade, out of rough unhewn stones and rubble, about the height of a man, some ten yards in front of the gate. It would not prove much help to them.

The Hebrews had built a wooden ramp, and during the night it had been silently brought close to the gate, to be propped up on the town side of the barrier. The barrier was to be turned to the Hebrews' advantage by giving the battering ram a downhill run at the doors.

The eastern sky was starting to grow lighter, and everything was ready. There were some messengers still scurrying about behind them, but like most of the army Jeho was on edge waiting for the trumpet note. Probably the Ammonites were listening for it just as intently, he thought, but with very different feelings.

The trumpet sounded, high and clear. A shout went up from thousands of throats, and Jeho found himself shouting as well, just a bellow of defiance at the black walls.

Arrows whizzed down from the ramparts, and a volley of arrows answered back. Stones were being levered over the city walls - probably they were part of the city walls - crushing men around the ram. The ram struck the doors with a deep resonant thud, and the men dragged it back for another charge.

The door creaked viciously, encouraging the Hebrews: the ram plunged forward again and this time the door gave way. The ram lodged in the gap between the leaves of the door and immediately the gap was filled with bodies, the soldiers were swept forward in a press of men and the doors were forced wide open: on the other side Ammonites streamed forward too. Jeho saw a sword sweeping toward his head, parried: the swordsman fell. Jeho trampled him as he was swept on: another face appeared, this time Jeho thrust straight between his teeth, the shock jarring his arm. Then suddenly there were no Ammonites in front of him, except prisoners. The gate had been taken and Hebrews were fanning out on all sides to quell the resisters. Eleazar organised his company and led them to the palace, while Ammonites melted into doorways and obscure corners.

The sun was up now.

At this point the difficulty was not so much defeating the Ammonites as keeping control over the victorious army. Men who have been fearful for their lives and suddenly find that they have survived and have a chance of spoil in front of them are very difficult to control. Men like Eleazar, Abishai and Benaiah were vital for maintaining the king's authority over his men.

Suddenly a group of Ammonite soldiers sprang out of a doorway. There were only about ten of them, but they fought like madmen. Benaiah's company took them on, forcing them back towards the house they had emerged from, but with Hebrews now in their rear. None of the Ammonites was taken prisoner: none of them had intended to be.

The episode had done nothing to make the Hebrews feel more tenderly towards the Ammonites. Even Ammonite soldiers who threw down their weapons immediately had to expect rough handling. Anyone who failed to drop his weapons was speared on the spot. Before long the women would be coming out, looking for a recognisable face, struggling to recognise the body of a husband or son, in the sudden realisation that life had changed forever.

The Hebrews were beginning to draw up in some sort of order after the fighting: David had summoned his senior commanders in front of the palace. Eleazar recognised Benaiah and Joab among other captains. The prisoners had been disarmed.

An Ammonite snatched a spear from the Hebrew beside him and drew back his arm. "Death to David!" he shouted, flinging the spear with deadly force. Benaiah flung himself forward but was too far away to reach the king in time. Another body met the spear's force: the body of a Hebrew soldier who stepped into line and intercepted the strike with his own breast. The spear entered two handsbreadths deep, and the soldier fell onto his knees.

Benaiah sprang up and swung his sword in an explosion of his colossal strength. The Ammonite's head thumped against the wall and rolled unevenly down the steps.

Eleazar reverently turned over the body of the dead Hebrew and drew out the spear.

"Palti, son of Laish, has given his life for his king."

David jerked as though he had indeed been hit by the spear. He instantly regained his composure.

The morning after the battle there was no shortage of urgent tasks: burying the dead, tending the wounded, arranging the food supply for the town's inhabitants. Jeho soon felt that he had made the easy transition from soldier to administrator. There was one administrative exercise that the army looked forward to above all else, however: the division of the spoils.

Trusted men carried out the contents of the Ammonite treasury and heaped it before the palace steps that Jeho remembered so clearly. A square of soldiers stood guard around it, facing outwards. Heralds called on the citizens to bring out their gold, silver and precious stones to be added to the pile, and on the soldiers to add anything they had taken overnight from the palace or the citizens.

At last the division began, starting with king David in person, who took the crown of the Ammonites from the head of Hanun himself. Its weight was a talent of gold, and it was set with precious stones. Then the Three and the Thirty had their turn, followed by the captains and officials and finally the common soldiers by tribes.

A different kind of spoil was represented by the beautiful, tear-streaked faces of the Ammonite women who would be taken west to new homes.

Jeho had not neglected himself in the distribution of the spoil: Caleb was weighed down with gold chains and jewellery, much of which was intended for Deborah.

Eleazar had acquired a blue-eyed, yellow-haired beauty who must have come from some land far to the north. She was only the second such Jeho had ever seen. She had probably had an unusual amount of misery in her short life to that day, Jeho imagined, but at least she had now been brought to the house of a better man than most. He wondered what Rebecca would say about the new member of her household.

The possibility of winning wealth on this scale was one of the factors holding the army together, Jeho knew well. What makes a man leave his farm, his wife and children, to face the possibility of death and the certainty of danger, discomfort and hard work in a foreign land? Partly the expectations of friends and family, partly a wish to serve the king, but also the chance of coming home with gold rings and serving-girls.

Jeho had been pulled up sharply by the sight of a girl with large, almond-shaped eyes, almost black in colour. A moment's reflection persuaded him that Deborah would not value her as an addition to the household. Jeho let her go to Benaiah on condition that he got one of the last donkeys in Rabbeh - most of the beasts had met the usual fate of livestock in a besieged city.

The thought of Deborah made Jeho realise how anxious he was to get home. He would have to get a message to her that he was unharmed - the slight burn he had received on his right arm from brushing against a cooking pot in camp could hardly be classed as a battle scar - and follow it as soon as he could.

First there was someone he wanted to see. Hanun's chamberlain might be able to give them a lot of useful information about the kingdom. A soldier from David's guard had heard a rumour that Ebom was dead: Jeho hurried through the palace to the upper suites.

Ebom had been cut down, but even without the rope round his neck it was obvious from the purple face and protruding tongue how he had died. Jeho thought of the anger that had distorted Ebom's fat face when he had condemned him and Eleazar as spies, and how his violence had been turned against himself at the end.

There was an overturned stool on the floor. Ebom must have stood on the stool to fix the rope to the lamp bracket in the ceiling, and kicked it away when he was ready. He had not given himself a long enough drop, so he would have been strangled to death by the rope. There was some soil on the floor under the lamp bracket. The robe he had died in was a fine blue silk one with red tassels along its bottom edge: his chain of office was still around his neck.

The chamberlain had destroyed some papers before he died, and other things as well. There were some burnt scraps of leather that had fallen out of a brazier, and a piece of wood that might have been one end of a pole or staff.

Jeho took the piece of wood, without quite being sure why. He gave orders for Ebom to be buried.

There was to be a work programme for the Ammonites: they were set to labour with saws and with iron picks and axes. The temple of Moloch was demolished, and its bricks were to be stockpiled for reuse. All the Ammonites, from Rabbeh, from towns and villages, were to be included in the work programme, making bricks and rebuilding.

David and his army returned to Jerusalem.

י

YOD

The tenth letter of the Hebrew alphabet

Your hands made me and formed me; give me
understanding to learn your commands.

Eleazar thought that the king had been behaving strangely since
Nathan's denunciation of him, at least towards him. He had seen
the king's eyes resting on him more than usual, and he thought
he had seen some evidence of displeasure. So he was not
surprised when a servant summoned him to the king's presence
on the morning after they had returned to Jerusalem.

Even if the king dismissed him, he could leave Jerusalem and
look forward to a quiet life on his estate. He had enjoyed his
service, but he could not blame the king for questioning his
loyalty. He had after all gone to Nathan with his suspicions. For
a fanciful moment he imagined the king ordering him to be
taken out for execution but then he thought that after such a
public repentance David could hardly do that.

"You will face no punishment, Jehoshaphat. My sin, even now
when it is uncovered, remains my sin and not that of the
discloser. I must know the truth, however: did you tell the
prophet of this?"

"I wouldn't have found out myself but for a coincidence. Your
new servant had the same name as my father. If he'd been called
Joshua or Joseph or Jonathan I wouldn't have given him a second
thought. But I was bound to take an interest in Ahilud."

"What you wrote in the letter to Joab must have been "kill this
messenger", wasn't it? Except Joab couldn't just take him out
and have him beheaded, because he'd done nothing wrong and
he was one of the Thirty as well. So you set him in the forefront

of the hottest battle and got him killed by the Ammonites. And do you know what preys on my mind most of all? It wasn't just Uriah who was killed that day. There were other men whose names won't go into the court chronicles because they weren't members of the Thirty. But they were sons and brothers and fathers, and you sent them to their deaths to cover up your adultery."

"There's something I want you to understand, Jeho." The king took a deep breath and looked down for a second. "I know that this is what people will say about me after all my works are forgotten, almost. People will remember me as the slayer of Uriah after they've forgotten that I slew Goliath. But that was not what struck me deepest. What struck me deepest was that the Everlasting turned away from me." He was looking Jeho straight in the eyes now, and Jeho knew that the king was speaking sincerely.

"I sinned against the Lord, Jeho. That was why I was relieved that Nathan laid bare my sin. At least now I am restored as the sheep of his pasture, whatever may happen to my family after my time."

"What will happen to me, lord king?"

"I have a job for you. I need a governor for Rabbeh. You can rebuild the city where you were dishonoured as you wish to see it."

Jeho was staggered. He was effectively being being offered the throne that Hanun had occupied when he and Eleazar had bowed before him, half a lifetime ago as it seemed.

Rabbeh of the Ammonites. What could he build on the site of the temple of Moloch? With the resources of a whole country he could do anything - establish a collection of books, perhaps, that would be the envy of the world, or gardens like nothing seen before.

The city where he was dishonoured, indeed. Jeho remembered the kicks and blows as he and Eleazar staggered through the streets. His face burned and his insides churned even after all he had seen since. The humiliation was nothing compared to the war that had followed it, but still it was much more personal.

Months before Jeho had told Deborah that what he wanted was to help David make something that counted for the service of the Everlasting.

"The king wants me to go to Rabbeh. He wants me to be the governor."

"To go to Rabbeh as governor? It's a great honour."

Jehoshaphat could see that something was troubling her.

"It isn't what you want, is it?"

"I know it would be a wonderful life in many ways, being the wife of the governor. I would be almost like a sort of minor queen."

"And yet perhaps that isn't what you want, is it? Perhaps it isn't what I want either. Here we have friends like Eleazar. There we would be surrounded by people who hate us. You would need armed guards every time you went out."

"It would be an enormous step up the ladder for both of us. I think our life is more than climbing a ladder. We have to enjoy the steps."

Deborah put her arms around his neck. They both knew what they wanted. They would find it together in Jerusalem.

Sometime later Deborah had the impression that Jeho's thoughts were on someone else.

"You are thinking about the king, aren't you?" Jeho agreed.

"The king says he has sinned against the Almighty."

"Of course he has - not to mention Uriah and the army, and Bathsheba for that matter."

"That's just my point. He says he has sinned only against the Almighty. As though the rest didn't count. I find it hard to understand."

"So do I, but I can see something of what he means. I think that the Everlasting has touched his life in a way that few others have known. He has made - will make - something that will stand for all time. So even his wrongdoing is wrongdoing against the Everlasting - not something that just leaves Him out of the picture. Does that make sense to you?"

"What is it that the Almighty wants of us? Does he want us to conquer other nations, to convert them, kill them or live in peace with them?"

Deborah frowned.

"I don't think any of that should be our priority. We have to get ourselves in good order first. Perhaps if the day comes when the law is really obeyed from end to end of the country, when the Almighty is honoured in every town and family, when there is no stealing or cheating or oppressing the poor then it might be time to turn our attention to other countries. But perhaps I'm just saying how I would like things to be."

Jeho couldn't be silent.

"That's not enough. We have to relate to them in some way. At the most basic level, they have things to sell that we want to buy: we have things to sell that they want to buy. And we can't ignore countries that come across our borders to raid and kill, or even countries that stop us from trading with our other neighbours."

Everyone thought of the war that started over the mistreated ambassadors. Silence fell. Eleazar and Jeho held each others' gaze. Had the war been worth it? Jeho knew of no scales in which to weigh that question.

Jeho was starting to wonder whether there could have contacts between Jerusalem and Rabbeh before, or even during, his unsuccessful embassy there. The man who could help him, he decided, was the king's secretary.

Seraiah was a rather self-important man. Jeho followed etiquette by sending Caleb to consult Seraiah's servants and arrange a meeting. It was a pleasant surprise that Seraiah offered an immediate meeting. After an exchange of courtesies Jeho came to the point:

"How would you send a message to someone without anyone intercepting it?" The secretary leaned back in his chair and considered the question.

"A complete guarantee against the message's disclosure is not possible, in my view. There are several possible approaches, but all have their flaws. Would you like me to give you some examples?"

"Of course."

"The most obvious way to send your secret message - apart from taking it yourself - is to send a trusted messenger. But such a messenger could be bribed, captured and tortured, seduced or plied with wine. Torture, by the way, is less reliable than most people think in uncovering the truth, and the last two are even worse. Another possibility is to use some kind of written message, but that can be even worse if it miscarries. Some courts use a technique with two messages: one is better hidden than the other, which is meant to be found. The idea is that once the enemy has found one hidden letter he will stop looking."

"How would the well-hidden one be hidden?"

"Again, there are different techniques. You can put a parchment in a stoppered flask in a wine-jar, for example. But my favoured technique - although I'm not sure I should be telling you this - is to hide something in plain view."

"For instance..."

"Write the message on the inside of a belt. Quick and easy."

" If the message is on the inside of a belt, surely it can easily be found?"

"Let me show you how it works. Give me your belt, Jehoshaphat."

Jehoshaphat took off his belt and handed it over to Seraiah.

"Pass me the chair in the corner."

Jehoshaphat fetched the chair and handed it to Seraiah who to his surprise placed it on top of his table.

"The problem that you have identified is that if I simply write my message on the inside of a belt as it is, then anybody who knows Hebrew letters can read it. So this is what I do."

Seraiah wound the belt around a leg of the chair, taking care to wind it so that there were no gaps. Jehoshaphat understood straightaway.

"So the recipient of the message has to have an identically sized piece of wood in order to get the sequence of letters right?"

"Yes. Someone who intercepts the message may be able to see that there is a message, but is not able to read it."

Messages had been passed between the chamberlain and Ahithopel by means of leather strips would around identical staves. He thought about the staff that Ahithopel had with him every time he saw him.

The chamberlain burned his staff, and then he killed himself. The suicide could be understood - he had no reason to expect mercy - not with Eleazar and Jeho at the king's side. Why burn the staff, then?

The stump left of the staff was a little shrunk and blackened, and it was just smaller than Ahithopel's. Jeho was certain that they had originally been exact matches. He remembered the remains of leather strips in the fire. They could have been the messages themselves, perhaps serving as sandal straps or harnesses.

Jeho remembered that at one time he had suspected Seraiah of being in league with Ahithopel, but he no longer thought so. Surely no-one who had been implicated in passing messages to the Ammonites could discuss the matter so dispassionately.

The Gadite farmer had told him of a lone rider that had passed east a day before them but never returned. If that was Ahithopel's messenger, he would have taken the most direct route to Rabbeh, but a roundabout route back to avoid meeting them. Jeho had more sense than to mention the farmer in any circumstances that could get back to Ahithopel. The farmer had done him nothing but good and he did not want to put him between Ahithopel and safety.

Without the farmer the evidence was unimpressive. There was only a charred wooden stump that might have matched Ahithopel's staff when it was whole.

Jeho remembered the night after the entry of the ark, when he had been lured out of his house for an appointment with a bowman. Someone had set out to kill him that night, and it was Ahithopel. He was certain: there was an indirectness about the whole scheme that fitted Ahithopel's character, but there was even less chance of proving that than his involvement with the coded messages. He still had the potsherd, but there was no way to connect it to Ahithopel. It was hardly likely that the rest of the pot would still be in his house, or that he would allow a search for it even if it were.

Ahithopel had lost the vineyard. Jeho had gained an enemy.

Ahithopel was still on the way up in terms of court politics. He was now the grandfather of the king's newest and to all appearances favourite wife. That provided him with a family connection to the king as well as his political link, and there was no doubt that he would exploit it. Ahithopel was a more dangerous man to cross now than he had ever been.

ת

TAW

The twenty-second letter of the Hebrew alphabet

May your hand be ready to help me, for I have chosen
your precepts.

The day had come for Caleb to be released from his service. He had some surprising news for his master.

"Master Jeho, it is not my wish to leave your service."

"Do you know what you are saying, Caleb? Do you understand that if you remain in my service it must be for life?"

"I do understand it, Master Jeho. I wish for no other life than to serve you and yours."

"Caleb, I can't accept this. When I first met you in Tyre I meant only that you would serve me for a term of years. I can't possibly merit being your master for life."

"Don't try to change my mind, master Jeho. I just want to know that my master is a good servant himself. I think there's more chance of that with you than with anyone else."

Jeho smiled as his servant and gripped his shoulder.

"And for my part I could wish for no better servant."

He thought a moment: "We'll need witnesses for this. Go to Nathan and Eleazar and ask them to come here tomorrow at the first hour."

The next day Eleazar and Nathan arrived in good time: when all were ready they went and stood outside the house's front door. A crowd was gathering, anticipating the rarely-seen ceremony.

"Caleb," began Jeho, "Your time of service is at an end, if you wish. Do you wish to be emancipated from my service?"

"Jehoshaphat son of Ahilud, I have no wish to leave your service. I am your servant to the end of my days."

"Then you will be known as a servant of the pierced ear."

Caleb stood by the doorpost. Jeho took the bradawl, held Caleb's ear against the doorpost and twisted the tool through Caleb's ear into the wood. Caleb winced with the pain, but the ceremony was quickly over. The two men embraced while the blood flowed, and Eleazar produced a cloth to bandage Caleb's ear. He whispered into it, so that only the three of them heard.

"That is the best choice you have ever made, Caleb."

As they entered the house Deborah drew him to one side. She closed the door on the celebrations. Deborah said, "There's something I have to tell you."

Her face was set but her eyes betrayed joy.

"You're going to be a father."

Jeho felt as if he could not grasp what she was saying. He tried to speak but no words came.

"Yes," said Deborah, "I am with child."

Jeho embraced her and thought a hundred thoughts in a second. He wanted to ask if she was sure, but she was ahead of him.

"No doubt at all."

There had been so much death, now there was life.

"I don't know how to take care of you now."

Deborah held him tighter.

"Just keep on treating me as you always do, as the best of husbands."

Would the child be a daughter, to take captive men's hearts and inspire poetry? Or a son to fight the king's enemies or lead embassies to far-off lands? Whichever, he would want to be a fitting father to his child.

This was a turning point in their lives, he realised. Nothing would be the same again, and it was the start of a greater adventure than the conquest of Rabbeh.

There was a celebration that evening. As the wine passed round, Rebecca and Deborah were sharing a joke. Jeho was still slightly surprised at how well they got on. He reflected that his closest friend was the bluff soldier Eleazar, so there was little enough reason to wonder at that.

"Let's go up to the roof, Eleazar."

The moon was just past full. They leaned over the parapet and looked towards the palace.

"Ahithopel talked to me once - before the Ark was brought here - about how costly war is. He said that the costs were certain and the gains uncertain, compared with trade. I didn't really understand then what he was talking about."

"It makes sense to me. Some victories are so dearly bought that it might have been better not to start the fight at all. But the loser pays even more."

Jeho thought of the Ammonites waiting to be taken into captivity on the morning Rabbeh fell. Ladies who had run their own households had been reduced to slavery, or at best to becoming unwilling wives to soldiers from another land who would take them away from everything they had known. He thought of Ebom hanging from a rope in his bedchamber, and of Hanun surrendering his crown to David. Certainly the losers paid most.

What had the campaign cost him, he wondered. He had known humiliation, pain and rough conditions. He had put his life at risk in battle, even if he had come out of it unscathed. The joy Deborah had given him outweighed all that. What the war had cost him perhaps was his relationship with the king. Neither he nor David would look at each other in quite the same way again. Was that mostly David's fault? Probably, but that was not really the point. The point was that the relaxed relationship had gone. He was not the only one: many others would see their king differently now. There might be difficult times ahead.

"You think that the king is holding the kingdom together because he won the war. It's the other way around. He won the war because he was the one meant to hold the kingdom together. But now things will be different. Keep your sword sharp, warrior."

"I always have kept it sharp, Jeho. At least that won't change."

www.ingramcontent.com/pod-product-compliance
Lightning Source LLC
Chambersburg PA
CBHW072000170626
46813CB00005B/1939